The Secret Lives of Ancestors

A California Pioneer Saga

Book One

AMYLEE

Also by AmyLee

Bird with a Bright Object: poems
More Bright and Shiny Things: a book of poetry

Copyright © 2024 by AmyLee

All rights reserved.

No part of this publication may be reproduced, distributed, or transmitted in any form or by any means, including photocopying, recording, or other electronic or mechanical methods, without the prior written permission of the publisher, except as permitted by U.S. copyright law.

This book is a work of fiction. The author makes no claim to be a historian or expert in the events described herein. This fictional story follows the ancestors of the author as closely as possible. While the main events in the story are based on actual events in history, some characters, storylines, names, places and dates are fictional products of the author's imagination.

The Timbers of This House, by Cordy Sander, copyright 1986, research used with the author's permission.

Cover Artwork and Design by Katherine Magpie Design

Interior Design by Jourdan Dunn

Table of Contents

Dedication
Preface
Acknowledgements

Chapter 1	Conversation with Marilla	1
Chapter 2	Go West – 1851	7
Chapter 3	The Journey Begins	17
Chapter 4	St. Joseph, Missouri – Fort Kearney, Nebraska	25
Chapter 5	Fort Kearney – Fort Laramie, Wyoming	39
Chapter 6	Fort Laramie – Fort Hall, Idaho	53
Chapter 7	Fort Hall – California	61
Chapter 8	Stony Point	79
Chapter 9	Christmas at Stony Point	89
Chapter 10	Tomales Dreams	97
Chapter 11	Mister and Missus	117
Chapter 12	The Widow	131
Chapter 13	Forgiveness	141
Chapter 14	Mount Shasta and Beyond	155
Chapter 15	Rules of Engagement	171
Chapter 16	Conversation with Abby	185
Chapter 17	Wedded Bliss	191
Chapter 18	Conversation with Mildred	207
Epilogue		211

Author's Note
About the Author

This book is dedicated to my Woodworth ancestors.
Love and loyalty.

Acknowledgements

My deepest gratitude goes to the many who have come with me on this journey. Your help arrived from astonishing places and changed my life forever. Thank you all so very much.

Linda Whalen - research, voice of reason, road trip partner, beta reader, and best big sister.

Linda Abernathy - for sharing your fascinating research on the 1915 Pan Pacific World Exposition.

The Sonora Writers' Group - for the continued support, boosts of my confidence, and encouragement.

Joanne DeEds and Trisha Ristagno - for sharing your considerable knowledge of horses.

Caitlyn - your support means the world to me.

The first cousins - Cordy, Diana, Elinor, RJ, Charlie - my gratitude to you all for sharing your memories and stories. I love you, sweet souls.

Mom and Uncle Bud - love you, miss you. Give my love to everyone on the other side.

My Woodworth ancestors - without you, this story wouldn't be possible.

Eric - for your patience and for making my work area a wonderful place.

Susan - for opening my eyes to other worlds.

Rick Holeman - for your words of encouragement and kindness always.

Dave Thompson - for always being an encouraging voice when I needed it.

Cousin Floyd - for your time and efforts.

Developmental Editor, Nicky Lovick (UK) - for pointing me in new and better directions.

Line Editor/Proofreader, Amanda Hallman - for your diligence and gentle care with my words.

Cover Design - Kat of Katherine Magpie Design - for your artistry and patience.

Interior Design - Jourdan Dunn - for your sense of style and patience as I make my way through the process.

Preface

My great-great-great-grandparents came to California desperate for a better life. They had no choice but to make whatever success they could, and the directive for survival was more potent than their fear of the unknown. How I wish I were that brave.

Pick Queen Anne's lace on the side of the highway, wade in the surf, and contemplate the generations of families who set crab pots and cast fishing nets. Imagine your ancestors collecting driftwood for the bonfires that would warm their bones as the waves raged and the wind gusted off the water. There are stories in each grain of sand where earth and sea collide.

There are vistas so filled with magic that even the most jaded can envision being transported back to a time before fields and hilltops were overwhelmed by modern life.

These moments and places have significance beyond points of interest on a map. They represent the memories and dreams of many. Listen as my ancestors whisper to you; allow them to cast their spell.

I was not the first to fall in love with this rough country; the elemental pull began generations before I was born. There is a belonging and homecoming that resonates from the hills and a song of rushing movement from the oceans, rivers, and streams. Each beat of my heart reverberates with the buffeting winds off the coast, and the salt air fills my lungs.

This wild land is in me.

Parmenus & Marilla
Woodworth
(1806 – 1878) (1807 – 1883)
|

Sandy
(1828 – 1898)
Darius
(1830 – 1907)
Martha
(1832 – 1902)
Abijah
(1837 – 1930)
Liza
(1843 – 1932)
Samuel
(1851 – 1924)

Chapter One
Conversation with Marilla

Everything I experience—smells, textures, and sounds—is filled with life and begs the question, am I awake or asleep? Whatever my state, I am here, in my great-great-great-grandmother's kitchen. A gentle breeze fills the lace curtains. I watch as light streams through rippled window glass and delicate shadows cast dancing patterns.

There is a precipice, and I stand at the threshold. My damp hands clench, heartbeat quickens, and excitement rules me. I worry that even the act of breathing may ruin my dream. I must speak with her, hear her voice.

Marilla loads the stove with wood to build up the fire. The smoke fills the kitchen with an acrid haze before it travels up and out the flue. The fuel ignites with pops.

Her movements are slow and filled with measured grace as she crosses the time-worn floor. Her long hair is swept up on her head in a once-tidy bun, but now wavy tendrils of auburn and gray have escaped and tumble down her broad back. The pattern of Marilla's dress under the apron is familiar—it sparks a memory, and I recognize the design. It is the MacDonald plaid of her family, and I've seen it many times in daguerreotypes and sepia-toned family photographs. Now I see that brilliant blue and green wool field, and I gasp.

She turns to me. I've interrupted her work, but she smiles. Marilla Woodworth looks tired after a long day, but her expression is kind, beckoning. I am both a stranger here and beloved family.

"Grandmother. Hello." My words are soft and hesitant. I do not want to break the spell.

"Hello to you, lass." Her voice is easy with the hint of a Scottish burr. She appraises me steadily. My presence doesn't seem to rattle her.

I'm not sure how much time I'll have with her, so I get straight to the point. "Will you let me get to know you? Will you tell me about yourself?" I pause, waiting for permission to continue, but she remains silent. "I need your stories. I'm writing about the family." I try to temper my enthusiasm, but I can't quite get over the idea that I am in her presence and she is from another time.

I wonder what's going on in my brain that this could occur. When it's over, will I be okay or discover I've completely lost my mind?

Marilla pauses in her work and looks at me as though entertaining visitors from the future is a common occurrence. A calm descends upon me, and I feel like I'm doing precisely what I should.

"I am here for you, Granddaughter. I understand this may feel strange."

"Is it magic?"

"Perhaps. It certainly has never happened to me before. But I believe you are here and that we are speaking. We've heard echoes of your voice; we know what you want."

A chill runs down my spine; I wrap my arms around myself in comfort and gather my thoughts. No matter how friendly I believe her to be, the enormity of dreaming her into existence is a lot to take in.

"We?" I squeak.

"Yes, our family." She stares thoughtfully at me, hands on her hips. After a moment, she resumes her work. Her delicate brow furrows in concentration as she moves to the large table and measures ingredients into a bowl.

My grandmother plucks an unasked question out of my head: "Biscuits. Please sit down." I seat myself, grateful the chair has substance, and I don't fall backward. She moves a glass jar filled with fresh herbs out of the way to the windowsill over the sink.

She watches me. Her image flickers in the dim light, and I feel the merest hesitation on her part. "We must know—we wonder if you are a wise woman, a witch?" I stare back at her in surprise. Something in the way she says it lets me know she wants my answer to be yes.

She wipes floury hands on the edge of her apron. Her eyes twinkle, and she projects images of the young girl she once was, the gentle mother, the patient wife, and the doting grandmother, all layered one upon the other, like living photographs. I like this trick.

Before me, she works the dough into a ball, sprinkles flour, and rolls it out flat. She uses a round metal cutter, and I have an intense urge to taste what she's made.

I'm still thinking about what she asked. Am I a witch? "I don't think I have any special gifts, but I guess I don't really know. I suppose I might have called you here. Maybe that is my power? I have had visitations from others in the family—long gone, but nothing quite like you. So I believe what's happening here is special. What do you think?"

"Hmm. Perhaps I summoned you to me," she challenges, her mouth quirking at the corners.

"I'm not alone in wanting to know the family. We are a curious bunch."

She nods but remains quiet.

"Maybe we found each other," I reply. "You are not just history to me or a name on my family tree." I place my hands on my heart. "I carry you with me, deep in my marrow. I know you feel it, too."

"Whatever you may be, it's pleasing to know someone still has a tenderness for us old ones." Marilla slides the pan of biscuits into the oven. My grandmother fusses and cleans up after herself. She runs her fingers over everything with care and love. I wish she would touch me—that I could embrace her.

"Child, I am long dead, but I've heard voices from the family, yours being the most persistent. I heard you calling, waking me."

The biscuits are almost ready. The smell envelops me and reminds me of other women in my life—other kitchens. "Granddaughter, I will tell you everything I know about the family. I asked if you are a witch, not because it frightens me, but because I wondered if you had some of my gifts."

I sigh. "I wish I did, but I'm not sure."

Marilla takes the biscuits from the oven and sets them on a plate to cool. "I knew many things from my grandmother, and she from hers, and so on back through time." Her eyes stare into the distance, and I can almost feel her searching her memories as she selects the stories to share with me. "My line of women all had a particular affinity with the natural world. Strange how the gifts skipped over my daughters.. Abijah, though, he could intuit the fine balance of nature and was an accomplished dreamer. Granddaughter, I think you are a dreamer, too, and these dreams are your magic."

God, I hope it's true. My obsessive brain works overtime thinking of everything she'd told me. If I suddenly awoke, would she be lost to me? I beg the universe to let me hear my grandmother's stories. "I've often thought how strong my pioneer ancestors must have been. I wonder if I could have done what you did. How brave you were to take that treacherous journey."

"No one knows what they are capable of until they are tested. There were nights I was filled with fear. What choice did I have but to keep going the best I knew? My husband had the word of the Lord to guide him, and I followed my husband without hesitation. But understand me, child, my faith was tested many times. There were days when I wondered if perhaps Parmenus misunderstood what God intended."

"Tell me everything," I beg.

Grandmother looks at me, and I see the distant past in her eyes. "Our story is far-reaching. Are you prepared, lass?"

Chapter Two
Go West - 1851

Every day, Marilla Woodworth prayed her eldest boy, Sandy, would come home safe from the war. Now she watched and wept as he rode up to where she stood waiting for him. He dismounted his horse and she cried out, "Oh Sandy, you're home, you're safe."

He embraced her, looked her in the eyes, and smiled. "I'm so thankful to see you, Ma. I wasn't sure this day would ever come. How is everyone? Where's my baby brother? Where's Pa?"

"He'll be here soon. He's mending the southern fence. Come in and let me feed you. Supper isn't ready, but I'll give you something to hold you over." She took the measure of her boy and saw the tightness around his eyes, the care-worn exhaustion on his face. War did that to a man. He was thin and needed good home cooking. She hoped to get him settled before the rest of the family descended.

Sandy dropped his dusty trail-worn saddlebags on the porch and took a closer look at the homestead. Those blue eyes of his never missed a thing, and Marilla wondered if the old place looked as worn out to her son as it did to her. The farm had reached near-decay brought about by a lack of cash and not enough hands to make necessary repairs. "I"m alright, Ma, but I'd best tend to my horse." Said horse was busy nibbling clover by the fence. He whistled, and Dante's ears twitched as he ambled over to him.

Marilla watched her son's back as he made his way to the barn. "Don't linger. Come to the kitchen as soon as you've finished." A feeling of relief settled over her—her eldest was home.

During dinner, the family got reacquainted with Sandy and told him the highlights of what he'd missed since he'd been gone. There was plenty of news about the grandparents, crop failures, the war.

"You don't remember me, do you, Liza?" Sandy smiled at his little sister. He'd seen her watching him, but she looked away each time their eyes met. Now she stared down at her hands in her lap.

"Liza's shy. Until she isn't. She'll warm up to you," said Sister Martha. She put her arm around the little girl's shoulders and gave her a squeeze of encouragement. Martha whispered something in her ear and Liza smiled and nodded.

Sandy continued as though she was a willing participant. "You were only two years old when I left."

Finally, Liza grinned. "I'm eight years old now."

"I was gone a long time, wasn't I?"

Liza got up, went to his side, and put her arms around his neck.

The youngest Woodworth, Samuel, was not yet a year old and watched quietly throughout dinner. He was a good-natured boy and sat placidly on Mary's lap. Suddenly he became red in the face, grunted and then started fussing. Marilla looked toward her daughter, raised her eyebrows, and whispered, "Will you please, Mary?"

"Of course, Mama. Sammy, let's get you cleaned up."

When dinner was finished, Marilla caught her husband's eye. "I'm pleased to have my family together again." Sandy was seated to her right. He squeezed her hand and smiled.

"When you left us, you were just a young man, untried by the rigors of the world. Now you return from the Mexican-American War as a man of strength and character. Welcome home to you, Son," his father said with such pride from his end of the table. "Now, tell us about the wild West."

Voices swelled with excitement. Everyone spoke at once. "Tell us everything."

Sandy pushed his empty plate away and leaned his elbows on the table. He ran his hand over his eyes, and for a moment, it didn't seem like he would say anything.

"Don't much want to talk about the war," he began slowly. "Except to warn my brothers of the ferocity and terribleness of it. We were always hungry—nothin' good about grub on the trail. They fed us to keep us alive, to fight the war, and that was about it. The cold crept in and made itself at home in our bodies. Unless, of course, when we were sweltering in the heat. I watched, helpless, as good men and horses died in agony. The fear got into our eyes and our mouths. You could feel it and taste the brutality and the blood. It's there in the dark when I close my eyes. I pray none of you ever have to live with those killing thoughts." His last words ended in a harsh whisper. No one said anything for a moment. Sandy's sisters and brothers stared at him mouths agape. Marilla and Parmenus looked at one another, their sadness evident.

Marilla wished she could take away her son's pain. She would pray that his troubles be lifted. Perhaps being home and embraced by the love of family would be enough to heal him.

Just when Marilla was sure he wouldn't say another word, Sandy seemed to shake off the darkness. He took a deep breath and pressed on. "But, California is somethin' else. And I'll gladly tell you about it." Gone was the broken young man; now, his bright blue eyes sparkled with plans for the future.

"Let me dish up dessert. I made an apple crumble for you, Sandy." Marilla hurried into the kitchen while Martha and Mary cleared the table.

The day's heat was finally beginning to subside, and Marilla propped open the windows to allow fresh air to circulate. She heard crickets chirping in the gloaming of the June evening. A trail of sweat trickled down her back, and she stood in the stillness for a moment, grateful to feel the slight lifting of the oppressive humidity. She wiped her neck with the end of her apron and rejoined her family at the table.

Once everyone was served, Sandy resumed his tale. "When the treaty was signed in 1848, I was in that last skirmish down at Todos Santos. I finished my service and worked my way up the Pacific Coast. I wanted to see San Francisco and Gold Country. Seemed a waste to be in the area and not explore. So I took odd jobs, drove a stagecoach, shod horses, and even did some farm work for a man who needed an extra hand. Finally, I headed north through Petaluma, Tomales, and the Russian River. It was plain to me that this was where I wanted to call home, and I plan to go back. California's where a man can get a good start in life. Where hard work can lead to success and not disappointment and the misery of being poor." Marilla inhaled sharply in surprise and looked wide-eyed at her boy.

Parmenus' eyebrows shot up at his son's declaration. "What do you mean go back?" he demanded. Marilla watched her husband as the emotions quickly played over his face—curiosity, shame, hope, and confusion. Sandy was proposing something that he'd never considered.

"There's nothing here for me anymore. Or for any of us, in my opinion. Pa, you've worked all your life, struggled, and what do you have to show for it?" Parmenus looked as though he was going to interrupt, his eyes narrowed at his son's perceived insult, but Sandy continued. "Your expertise is wasted here. In California, a man of your experience is paid a decent wage. Our family could be successful. We could be respected members of a prosperous community there. California is just what our family needs, and it's where I intend to settle."

Marilla rose from the table, unshed tears threatening. She looked her son in the eye. "You're breaking my heart. Please don't leave us. Don't go."

Darius had been silent, taking in all of his brother's words. He sat and listened and watched. There was a battle of wills between Sandy and his parents. He felt the fire of excitement within himself; the possibility of going to California was the most important idea he'd ever entertained. And the yearning it brought about was almost too much to bear. He wondered if he could go with Sandy. If the rest didn't come along to California, he was afraid that he and Sandy would have to go against the family. Against Pa. He felt a tugging on his heart.

He didn't want to insult his parents, but he wanted to know what was possible. And he was determined to prove to Sandy he was on his side, encouraging him. "Tell us more, Brother. How can we make this happen?" Darius leaned forward and gave Sandy his undivided attention while out of view under the table, his knees bounced with nerves, and his heart pounded in his chest. Sandy's eyes narrowed for a moment assessing, and then the brothers grinned at each other. Even quiet Abijah was drawn in.

Pa coughed and captured his sons' attention. Face red, his voice cut through their excitement. "I can't run the farm without you boys."

Darius saw the look on his father's face and felt the disappointment of this new dream ripping from his chest. Pa was set in his ways. He was stubborn and expected obedience from his sons.

Moments passed in uncomfortable stillness. Their father sat, shoulders hunched, head down. He struggled for composure, and then said quietly, "I guess I need to hear more, Sandy. Abijah, Darius, I want you to come out to the barn with Sandy and me while the womenfolk get Sammy ready for bed." Ma looked as though she was about to argue but instead she sighed deeply.

Parmenus lit the lantern that hung by the front door and led the way with his boys close behind. As soon as they were in the barn, Sandy began to paint a dramatic and exciting picture of life in California.

"There are places on the West Coast where the weather is mild, the soil is fertile, and acreage is available practically for the taking. Our family could finally get ahead. We could prosper. There's work to be had for a man of your talents, Pa."

"Truth to tell, I've never been able to figure out why I couldn't be successful in Missouri or any other place, and it bothers me. I work hard for this family, so how is it that I have nothing to show for my labors?" Parmenus shook his head and his sons felt his shame.

"Pa, we know you done your best, always. But this is our chance to make something for the future. When the men in our family work together, we are stronger—we can accomplish anything. We'll help one another, as we always do, and we will prosper." Pa looked at each of his sons and saw men willing to take a chance. Darius let out a relieved breath; their father was convinced. He could feel it.

"Tell me what you know of prospecting, Sandy," encouraged Darius. "I read the streets are paved in gold," he wiggled his eyebrows, joking.

"It's chancy and a dangerous way to earn a living. The gold rush may have made some men wealthy beyond their wildest expectations, but it made a whole lot of others go bust, and those were the lucky ones. Many didn't get out with their lives. Gold fever seems to bring out the worst in men. I tell you, it is a curse more often than a blessing."

"Seems like an unreliable means of making a living," Pa grumbled.

"Well, not entirely," Sandy admitted. "There are large mining outfits in the Sierras, and a man could work for one and be paid a pretty penny. Of course, it's still hazardous, but you'd at least have the security of the men who own the mines behind you. That's how lots of fellows do it. But there are other ways to make a dollar."

"Alright, Son. You better tell us," Pa conceded.

Sandy's eyes glowed in the kerosene light, and Darius could feel how much his brother needed to make this dream come true. "I've got a little money saved, not much, but every bit will help. If we buy acreage, we can farm, raise livestock. The place I have in mind is near the ocean, and it is starting to come alive with commerce. When I traveled through, everywhere I looked, I saw new bridges, businesses, and homesteads. Pa could work on those projects while we boys begin our own concerns. With care and planning, there are many ways for us to begin."

Pa nodded, contemplating their lives ahead. "And there's your mother to be convinced." It wouldn't be easy to get her to agree, but she needed to understand that the family must go West. Nothing good would come of them staying in Missouri.

Abijah's eyes darted back and forth from his pa to his brothers as they spoke. All the while, he thought of opportunities and land. He was a different sort of person and he knew it. His family had always done their best to encourage him and not make him feel awkward or alone. Heck, it was difficult to ever be alone in a family with seven children. He loved them. Especially Pa, who'd taught him everything about building, farming, and taking care of livestock.

He also saw the respect his parents had for each other. The kindness and humor and true love—he wanted that someday for himself. He was a 14-year-old boy with a stutter, shorter than the other men in his family, he was all knees and elbows and bottomless pit at the dinner table. But Abijah had big dreams, and he knew his best chance at making a name for himself was in California. He'd heard stories and read articles about vast fortunes being won and lost. He firmly believed his way forward was out West, and he would do what he could to help make it possible for his family.

"I want to go to California. H...how will we do it?" Abijah grinned, and Sandy and Darius clapped him on his back. Pa ran his big hand over his head, mussing his hair.

"You'll be in charge of our livestock, Son. Out of all of us, you're the best with the animals, and I know we can count on you." Abijah felt his face grow warm at his father's praise.

Sandy crossed his arms over his chest and nodded his head. "Lots of work to be done, gents. I can lead us. I know the trails. It's time to make our plan."

Pa leaned against the big doorway to the barn. It was full dark now. There was a sense of purpose to him now that had long been absent. "I best go speak with your ma."

The house had finally settled for the night, and Parmenus and Marilla lay in the dark, whispering about the day's events. A three quarter moon had risen and cast a pale glow as they faced one another, careful not to awaken the little ones.

"Tonight was a fine time, wasn't it? Sandy's home safe."

"I know what you're going to say, Husband. About California and leaving our loved ones behind." Parmenus waited patiently for her to continue her thoughts. He knew she needed to work things out her own way and tried not to prod.

She took a deep breath before continuing. "It seems the way out West holds much to be desired, but I'm worried."

"My love, tell me what's in your heart." He caressed her cheek and took her hands in his, willing her to continue.

"California is very far away. I worry about the journey."

"We have plans to make and many things to decide. Tomorrow I will write to my father and tell him about Sandy and everything. He would never begrudge us our chance, and he will have much advice to offer."

"Parmenus, do you suppose our sisters and brothers would ever be courageous enough to embark upon a journey such as you and Sandy suggest?"

"We cannot know. We can only plan for what *we* will do." Being married this many years, he was careful to keep calm during negotiations with Marilla, and at this point, he couldn't tell if his wife was now closer to an agreement with him or if he'd set her further from his goal. What he knew was that he must pick his way forward with caution.

"And what if there's another child? What will we do then?" As the words were out of her mouth, Parmenus knew this was the true root of her concern.

He drew her closer and pressed a kiss to her forehead. "Don't be afraid, Marilla. You'll see; everything will come out right. Put your trust in me, and together with our children, we'll make this happen."

"I do trust you, but Parmenus, I can't think anymore tonight. We must sleep." And with that, his wife rolled to her side, and moments later, he heard her breathing change and knew she slept. Unfortunately, he was too wound up, and his mind wouldn't settle—too many ideas bursting forth. There was much he had to learn before his family left for California.

The following day, hoping she'd given their journey West more thought, Parmenus approached his wife while she prepared breakfast. He came up behind her, wrapped his arms around her waist, and rested his chin on her shoulder. She turned to face him, and he watched as a smile lit her face. Ah, he captured her yet again. Marilla would eventually agree to the move.

"And? What do you think, Wife?"

She gave her husband a quick laugh. "You are tricky, Sir. And we have many plans to make. Now sit down to a cup of tea, and I'll serve your breakfast when it's ready."

His wife was still apprehensive about uprooting the family, and he understood her worries about more babies. But still, he prayed fervently for California and hoped to God he could find a way to make it happen.

Chapter Three
The Journey Begins

Marilla stood and stretched. Her back ached and her hands were tired. Scrubbing canvas trousers on the washboard took strength and stamina. As the years passed, she noticed it was becoming harder for her to complete the task. Finally, when she'd finished, she laid the stiff clothing over the picket fencing that protected her kitchen garden and wiped the sweat from her brow on the sleeve of her work dress.

There was still snow on the ground under the trees, but for the end of March, it was unseasonably warm, and it felt good to be outdoors. It had been a hard winter, and Marilla decided to enjoy this brief reprieve of sunshine.

She drew a bucket of water from the well and filled the dipper that hung on the nail there. After she quenched her thirst, Marilla sat on the front steps to rest for a few minutes. Her eldest daughters, Martha and Mary, were preparing supper and keeping her youngest children out of mischief, so she had a rare moment to rest and think.

A pair of red-tailed hawks lifted and dipped to the west on gentle warm air currents; she heard their distinctive whistling calls. They must be searching for a nesting site. Marilla felt a pang of sadness that by the time the eggs hatched, her family would be long gone from the area.

She thought about the things she still needed to get done before her family left to go West next month and thought of the money Parmenus had received from his father. It came as a surprise, but they would use it to help pay for essentials they'd need for the more than five months on the trail. How strange it would be to have the money to purchase what they needed. Money had always been scarce, but with her father-in-law's gift and a frugal plan, they could get what they needed.

Parmenus approached and as he got closer, she could see how tired he was after working hard all day. He sat next to her on the steps. "What are you thinking, Wife? You look bothered."

"I'll tell you, but you're not going to like it. I'm thinking about everything that could go wrong on the way to California. I'm making sure I'll know everything I need to prepare for."

Marilla didn't want to cause concern just because she was worried, but her husband always knew what to say to make her feel better.

"You can tell me anything. What are you afraid of?" He squeezed her hand before bringing it to his mouth to kiss. Marilla scooted in closer and laid her head on his broad shoulder.

She let out a tired sigh. "You are right. My imagination gets the better of me. I worry one of our children will be crushed under the wagon wheels or trampled by the livestock. And what if we're attacked by Indians? I've read such terrible stories."

"Don't go borrowing trouble, Marilla. How can it be any more dangerous than life on our farm? We've lived through bad accidents and our fair share of frights and lived to tell the tales."

"We are at Mother Nature's mercy, and living so far from town, we've always had to rely on ourselves. This will be much the same, I suspect." Working things through with her man always felt right.

Martha shouted from the kitchen. "Ma, Samuel's crying for you! Do you want him, or should I try to quiet him?"

"See if you can settle him. I need a few more moments of peace."

"Alright. But you know he's going to cry for you." Marilla heard sounds of her daughter trying to convince the baby that Mama was resting. She heard Samuel's sweet piping voice reply and Martha's gentle laughter.

Marilla's thoughts now flitted back and forth between the goodbye letters she'd sent to her siblings and mother, and correspondence she'd received back from them. Over the years, they'd remained steadfast, but life and circumstance had caused the distance between them to grow. She sighed. *It is just the way of things, and no point in crying over something I can't help.* As she expected, they all wished her well. She would simply have to accept that she might never see them again in this life. It was a bittersweet time for her and Parmenus, too. Marilla wiped tears from her cheeks and remembered to be grateful that at least they had one another, their children, and the promise of a brighter future.

The Secret Lives of Ancestors

Last Fall, the kitchen was in constant use at harvest and even more so than usual in preparation for the journey. Marilla and her daughters dried and preserved the fruit and vegetables to get the family through the long winter and what the family would need for the months on the pioneer trail.

Marilla had gathered and dried even more bundles of herbs, as was her custom for seasoning, teas, tinctures, and salves. Over her life, she'd learnt the healing properties of many plants and how to use them medicinally. And now, she would have the opportunity to learn new remedies from the other women she hoped to encounter along the trail. She quizzed Sandy about the plant life out West, and intended to forage what she could as they made their way across the plains and through the mountains.

Parmenus and Sandy had signed on with a large group of folk traveling West. Mr. William Leffingwell was the group's leader in charge of the finances for the trip. His wife and daughter would accompany him, and Parmenus spoke well of their family.

"Marilla, I know you'll get on with Leffingwell's wife. Perhaps you two will become good friends."

It had been years since she'd had time for women friends. No one lived close enough and her children, husband, and the farm kept her busy. "I hope so. I expect we'll spend time together, cooking communally, washing clothing, and caring for the little ones."

Parmenus sold the homestead for the remaining cash he needed to help finance the trip. He'd hoped to get more for the old place, but it wasn't exactly a thriving concern, so he just thanked God and felt grateful. Most of what he owned wasn't worth taking with them, so he sold what he could, and on the last night in their old home, everyone slept on the floor in their bedrolls. e promised Marilla he'd build her a fine house and whatever furniture they'd need. He brought his hand tools, knowing he'd need them along the way, and Marilla had a few sentimental items that she didn't want to part with, but mostly, they were leaving for their new life with only the clothes on their backs.

At the break of dawn the following day, the wagons were loaded and the teams hitched. Abijah helped Sandy and Darius get their milk cow and calf hooked onto a short rope at the back of the smaller wagon. The chickens were settled in their willow baskets, but the upheaval made them nervous, and they clucked and pecked. A very confused young rooster crowed every few minutes.

Folks from neighboring farms showed up to offer last-minute advice and to wish them well on their new adventure. The Woodworth family headed out from their home for the last time, waving and crying their goodbyes until the last glimpse of the old farm disappeared from view around the bend.

Parmenus sat up front with Abijah in the covered wagon, with Martha, Mary, Liza, and Samuel bouncing around in the back. "Hang on, everyone," he directed and clapped his son on the back. "Let's go!" Abijah let out a whoop—he grinned from ear to ear.

Darius drove the farm wagon with Ma and the squawking chickens. "Do you suppose I've forgotten anything?" his mother asked, looking behind them.

He chuckled. "I don't know how you could—there's nothin' left to forget. It'll be okay, Ma, you'll see." Darius smiled but noticed the sad look on his mother's face.

"I know," she said. "Place was falling down around us—we'd be in a world of trouble next rainy season." Understanding their dilemma didn't make leaving any easier.

Sandy followed behind on horseback, checking to ensure everything was tied down tight. Darius turned in his seat, looked back at his brother, and tipped his chin to him.

The family arrived at the neighboring village mercantile, and Parmenus jumped down from the wagon. He was so excited to get started that he nearly lost his footing when he stumbled over a rock.

"Careful, Pa," Abijah called out.

"I'm fine, boy. Just anxious to get out there and get our journey started. Better watch myself, though." He wiped the sweat off his brow and chuckled.

Parmenus took his two oldest sons into the shop to settle their outstanding debt with the owner. The shopkeeper indicated their provisions that were stacked outside the front entrance, and so began the task of loading up the wagons. Sandy and Darius rolled and hefted the containers, storing them safely in the wagon beds, as Abijah helped check everything off the list. The number of provisions they needed for themselves and their livestock was staggering. Bacon, coffee, tea, saleratus, flour, vinegar, cornmeal, oats, hardtack, sugar, and rice were just a few of the supplies piled high in wooden barrels. Parmenus looked up and saw that their loaded-down wagons had the attention of everyone out in the early April morning. Folks stood by and watched as the many months' worth of food was carefully packed into the back of the wagons.

"Not much room to spare, is there?" Abijah noticed.

"It's going to be tight, that's for sure. Suppose most of us will be sleeping under the wagons." Parmenus scratched his head, trying to determine if everything would fit.

Martha stood by with Samuel. She grasped his hand tight and watched as her little brother's mouth opened in surprise. "What's that?" he asked.

"They're loading our supplies, little man," Martha assured him. "We're going to need all of it for our big journey. Won't it be grand, Sammy?"

Samuel pulled on her hand and tried to wiggle free. He wanted to get up close to watch his brothers as they worked in the morning sun, and Martha struggled to keep him safe and out from underfoot. "Come back here," she cried.

"I've got him, Daughter." Just as Samuel tried to make his escape, Parmenus lifted him up, and the little boy scrambled onto his pa's shoulders for a better view of the activity.

"Come on, boys, we've got to move out. Next stop, St. Jo." Parmenus waited for his family to settle before he signaled to Abijah to get those oxen moving.

Chapter Four
St. Joseph, Missouri to Fort Kearney, Nebraska

After more than two years of planning, in April of 1853, Parmenus and his family left St. Joseph, Missouri, in their covered wagon and smaller supply wagon. They joined a party of sixteen families for the six-month odyssey to California. Parmenus was 44 and his wife, Marilla, was 43; their seven children ranged in age from Sandy at 25-years-old down to the nearly three-year-old Samuel.

The wagon bumped along every rut and stone in the dirt track. Dust finer than flour coated the livestock, people, and every possession, and made its way into the sweat gathered at the back of Marilla's neck and everywhere else. At first she tried to keep up with the dirt by frequently using a damp cloth but gave up on the futile work after a few days. *We're all just going to have to be filthy until we can get a good wash in a creek.*

A half day's journey outside St. Jo, Marilla became painfully aware of how uncomfortable it was to ride in the wagon. *At least I'm not ready to give birth.* She laughed at herself and padded the seat with a folded quilt, then rolled up another to provide support at her back. Eventually, she'd get used to the jostling, but at the moment, there was only weariness on her first day of the journey West. Tonight, she'd ask Parmenus to rub her back with the rosemary and lavender salve she'd prepared with this very problem in mind.

As the miles wore on, Marilla watched Abijah with the team of oxen. He was so good with them, so gentle and kind. He kept hold of the yoke, and she watched him speak with them, whispering commands and praise. Although Marilla had complete faith in his skill with the animals, she continued to hold tight to the reins as though doing so would give her some semblance of control. She thought back to the day her husband told her about giving Abijah the burden of responsibility for the animals.

"It's a weighty task, Marilla, but he's 16 and practically a man. Sandy was 17 when he left for war." Then he reminded her that Abijah raised the team leads, Blue and Old Boy, since they were but a few days old. He'd bottle-fed and trained them patiently, and they obeyed his gentle but firm commands from the beginning. The other pairs came to him when they were yearlings. It took a bit longer, but soon Abijah had them working well with the first two.

"Alright, Husband, you know best. I know you'll keep your eye on him."

"He's stronger than you might imagine. When faced with adversity, Abijah thinks his way through every problem. I am convinced that our journey will build his confidence. I trust him."

Marilla tried her best not to favor any of her children, but there was always something special about Abijah. His intuitive mind was strong and she felt an affinity with her son's gifts. She saw it each time she looked at him, the way he used his dreams to strengthen how he moved through the world. He was a unique individual, and she looked forward to seeing the man he would become.

She supposed it came to him because of the stutter—as a little lad, he was teased when they'd go to town and at school, and it could have soured his personality, but it never did. His brothers and sisters tried to protect him, but the unkind words hurt Abijah. He was sensitive to other's feelings and behaviors.

His early experiences made Abijah a champion for those unable to stand up for themselves. Nothing got his blood boiling faster than to find someone weaker being taken advantage of.

Early on, Parmenus noticed his difficulties and began giving the boy more responsibility with the farm animals. The hard work and his father's trust built Abijah's confidence stronger than anything else. And when he'd told his son the role he'd play on the journey West, Abijah beamed with happiness.

Liza and Mary fussed with each other in the back of the wagon. Their shrill voices traveled up to where Marilla sat. She turned around for a moment and watched as they lay on their backs, arms reaching towards the canvas canopy as they played Cat's Cradle.

"Liza, scoot over; I'm squashed," Mary reprimanded.

"Quit hogging," Liza sassed. She jabbed her older sister in the side with her elbow, and Mary pinched the little girl who then screeched. Marilla interrupted them before their behavior escalated to tears.

"Girls, stop the bickering," she coaxed. *Lord help us, it's going to be quite a trip.*

No sooner had the girls finally settled down than Sandy approached on horseback. "Everything alright, Ma?"

"I'm fine—a little bit lost in my thoughts, passing the miles. Plenty of time to think while on the trail, isn't there?"

He nodded. "Just wanted to let you know, we'll make it an early night. Give folks a chance for rest." Marilla issued a silent prayer of thanks, and her son tipped his hat to her and rode back to the next group of wagons to check the travelers.

The pioneers took to the trail with a sense of optimism many had never before experienced. Some families were more affluent than others, but when it came down to it, everyone was looking to improve their circumstances. The joy of embarking upon their dream made for an idyllic first few days of travel. They reveled in the good moments and relied upon one another to get through the small hardships that occurred along the trail. The sheer beauty of the changing countryside served as a welcome balm against the exhaustion. Each day survived meant a day closer to their destination.

As the journey became more commonplace and took them further from everything they had once known, patience was tested. Their blistered feet were rubbed raw before calluses had the chance to build. Skin baked in the afternoon sun, shivers at night in the cold and bedding not so comfortable as what they left behind began to fray even the most placid tempers.

For the women and girls, time melded into one of constant motion and jostling, cowbells clanging, chores, and crying babies. Mornings began well before dawn for man and beast alike. The women cooked meals together to save time and energy, and it wasn't long before friendships were formed amongst the travelers.

"Mary, what do you like best about our journey so far?" Martha pulled her shawl around her shoulders against the evening chill. The sun had just dipped below the horizon, and the warmth of the campfire was inviting and cozy. The youngest children were bedded down and finally quiet, and those still awake were seated companionably on the supply crates.

Mary thought for a moment before she replied. "When we're off the trail for the day. I love the evenings. Once our chores are finished and we can sit quietly in the darkness. Just we two, free to talk about our dreams, our fondest wishes. I like to imagine we're the only ones out here when it's so quiet. We can look up to the stars and think about what heaven must be. And then I hear voices on the breeze, soft and low, and a twig snaps, and it's one of our brothers or parents." Martha nodded. "What about you?"

"Waking up in a new place every morning is like a miracle. At least, that's how I feel. How lucky we are to see this land, the mountains, the rivers, the valleys. But you know me, Mary, I get frightened at night. That's when I think about everything that could go wrong." The sisters were silent and watched the flames dance. The pop and snap of pitch and expanding wood cut through the night, and something in the nearby buck brush scrambled for safety—an owl hooted.

Martha gasped and whispered, "What was that?"

"Just an owl; nothing to be afraid of."

"That's the difference between us. You are brave and meet every challenge no matter the difficulty, and I fear the unknown and things that may never come to pass."

"I prefer to think that you are cautious, and I am sometimes too bold." She put her arm around Martha to comfort her.

"Crossing rivers gives me chills. I wish we could go another way." Marilla ladled more stew into her husband's bowl.

"I know. We'll be crossing at least one, and perhaps there will be more." He dug into his second helping and worked at it steadily. "That's good supper."

"River crossings are likely the most dangerous aspect of this trip, you know. I've read reports of death by drowning are not unusual, and I'm fearful because I don't swim."

"Marilla, the boys and I will ensure you won't be alone when you cross. You'll be on a barge or a raft with our supplies and float across as safely as possible." Parmenus tried to assuage her worries, but she had trouble believing things would be okay. When the feelings of fear became too much, she prayed fervently for strength.

The novelty of the journey had worn off and tempers flared amongst the pioneers. Opinions varied on how individual families were faring on this venture. Some took the changes in everyday life graciously, and others did not. Those in the latter group liked the secrets and whispered gossip on the trail and in the evenings. Sandy overheard plenty of complaints and tried not to let them bother him, but when the anger was directed toward him, it was almost more than he could bear. *Suppose they need someone to blame. That's the fear talkin'*, he mused. It was part of the responsibility of his job.

The Secret Lives of Ancestors

The wagons stopped an extra day to make repairs and tend to necessities that were impossible to solve when they constantly moved. A few ladies took advantage of the lull to get their washing done at a creek near their encampment. They performed the hard, hot work using lye soap and a scrub board, but the task gave them the perfect opportunity to visit with old and new friends.

One of the women looked at her red, cracked hands and shook her head in dismay. "Before I married, my hands were soft. Look how ugly they are. I can hardly stand it."

"All of our hands look about the same. Nothin' to be done about it, except maybe rub them with a little tallow if you've got it to spare," said the second woman.

There was a lull in the conversation, and the three looked up and acknowledged Marilla and Eunice Leffingwell who'd made it down to the river's edge with their baskets of clothing.

"Hello, ladies," greeted Marilla.

"Is there room for us to wash up too?" Eunice asked pleasantly.

"Of course. We're nearly finished, but we'll stay and visit a while if you don't mind. I'm Jenny. And this is Alice and Flora."

Marilla introduced herself and Eunice as they got busy with their wash.

Alice asked forwardly, "What do you think of our scout? Have you spoken with him? I sure hope he knows what he's doing."

Marilla's mouth curved up on one side, but she remained silent. Eunice shot her a look with raised eyebrows.

"I hope so, too," said Flora, the only single woman in the group. "He's mighty handsome and those blue eyes," she ended with a little sigh.

Finally, Marilla decided if she didn't say something quickly, things could become uncomfortable. "Ladies, that's my son, Sandy," she said with good nature. "And he does know what he's doing. Our journey is dangerous, but our chances of arriving safely are higher because of him."

"Oh, I'm so embarrassed." Flora's cheeks flushed. "Please don't say a word to your son. I'd about die if he knew."

Marilla smiled, "That's alright; I won't tell him."

Eunice laughed softly. "Sandy's been courting my Cyndi. Mr. Leffingwell and I expect he'll be asking for her hand in marriage any day."

"Well," Alice interrupted to try to save Flora's pride. "I've heard your son was in the war out West, and that's how he got the job. Is that true, Marilla?"

"My son has been from Missouri to California and back again. He knows the trails, and he'll keep us safe." Marilla nodded emphatically and saw the relief on the other women's faces.

Eunice rinsed a heavy work shirt in the river. She beat it on a flat rock and then swirled it in the cold water to get the soap out. "We are lucky to have a guide with so much experience. Some wagon trains come West with no expert guide looking after them. I don't want to imagine how frightening that would be."

Flora, Alice, and Jenny finished their washing and loaded the wet clothing back into their baskets. "We'd better get back to camp. Are you and Eunice nearly finished?" asked Alice.

"We'll be a while, yet. I've got the rest of the shirts to rinse. But why don't you come for a cup of tea some evening?" Marilla invited.

"Oh, that would be nice," said Jenny.

"All of you ladies are invited. It would be nice to have female companionship while the men have their weekly meetings."

"We'll come on Wednesday evening, Marilla," said Flora.

"Good day to you both. See you soon," said Alice as she joined the other two women making their way back to camp.

Marilla and Eunice worked together in silence for quite a while, scrubbing, rinsing, and wringing out the excess water. Finally, Eunice paused and looked up at her friend. "Tea will be a good chance to become friendly. Do you think they'll stop by?"

"I expect they will." Marilla wiped her wet hands on her apron and then gathered the laundry. "That's me, finished. Are you ready too?"

"Yes. Let's go back." Eunice offered a tired smile.

After dinner, Marilla took a rare few moments to relax. Parmenus came to sit beside her on some supply crates. She told him about meeting the neighbor ladies.

"I was surprised they didn't know about Sandy, and they had no idea he was my son. We've been so busy with travel that we haven't gotten to know anyone. That needs to be fixed."

"I agree. We'll do better if we know one another. Most folks are decent and hardworking, but I cannot lie; there are a couple of grouches in the group. They've been giving Sandy a hard time."

Marilla shook her head. No matter how good things were going, someone would always have objections. "They better not say anything to me about my son, or there will be trouble."

She leaned into Parmenus, glad for his strength and comfort. Marilla enjoyed their quiet conversations together and thought how nice it was to have a husband who wanted to know her thoughts.

Parmenus lifted their joined hands and kissed his wife's fingertips. They stayed that way for a few minutes before Samuel's cries signaled an end to their quiet time.

"Better check the children." Parmenus helped his wife up.

When Abijah saw his brother riding toward him faster than normal, he felt a moment of panic. Then he saw Sandy's expression and relaxed. He tried to keep as even a disposition as possible because, as his pa always reminded him, the animals sense when all is not right.

Abijah nodded a greeting, and Sandy dismounted and walked along, holding the reins, keeping a bit of distance between his horse and the lead oxen.

"Hey Brother, how are you this morning?"

"Couldn't be b...b-better. How're things with you?"

"I'm doin' alright. Thought I'd check in and make sure all is well with you."

"You're making sure I'm staying out of trouble," Abijah smirked.

Sandy raised an eyebrow, trying for a serious expression. "It's just the job, Brother. You're up here all by your lonesome. How's that going for you?"

"My animals are better than most people I know, present company excluded," he joshed. "Honestly, I'm happy up here. I get visitors a few times a day. That's good enough for me."

"I knew you'd be just fine up here at the front. You, Darius, and I are the leaders of our party." Sandy said it that soft way of his, but there was business behind his words.

"Hadn't thought about it that way. Thought maybe you were the one leading, and we was just followin' along."

"Well, I suppose so. But if something happens to me, then Darius and you will bring everyone through to California." Sandy's words weighed heavy on his younger brother. So many lives at stake—it troubled Abijah.

"That's some responsibility. Maybe we're better off tryin' to remain positive and not think about the worst that could happen."

"I hear you. But we still need to plan for the worst and pray for the best."

As the eldest, Sandy could be stern, but Abijah knew the compassion behind his brother's actions, and he respected him for all he'd accomplished. After all, he was responsible for the lives of each person in their wagon train.

"But Darius and I don't know the trails, and how will we negotiate with the different tribes? We need *you,* Brother." He'd had enough talk for now about trying to lead this band of strangers into the unknown. Abijah reached into his pocket and came out with half an apple he'd been saving for later. "And how about you, Dante?" He gently offered it to his brother's horse, and Dante deftly took the apple from Abijah's out-stretched palm.

Sandy let out a bark of a laugh. "You trying to steal my horse?"

"I'm just making friends. He's very smart, you know, and he knows who the best people are, don't you, boy?" Abijah stroked Dante's mane and raised a cloud of trail dust.

"We'll meet up after dinner, hear? I want to talk to you and Darius together."

"You know I'll be there. And you can count on me for whatever you need me to do. Promise you." Abijah supposed it was a good thing to be included in the plans. He just didn't want to think about anything bad happening to Sandy.

The oxen kept up their plodding pace, ignoring the other four-legged beast that seemed to want the attention of their caretaker. Abijah expected his brother to ride off to his next errand, but he kept walking alongside holding his horse by the reins. *Sandy probably needs the company as much as I do.*

"Did I ever tell you how we found each other?"

"What, you and Dante? Can't say you did."

Sandy patted Dante on the neck. "After the war, I found myself without a horse. I needed transportation home, and I met a man who needed money. He was selling a couple of horses. One of them was a mare; she was a beauty, but I couldn't imagine her getting me back home—she didn't have enough heart. The man said he'd sell me the gelding for a good price as he bit him every time he got too close. I looked him over and thought we'd make a good pair, and we got along just fine right from the start. And boy, could he go. The horse trader told me he'd named him Dante, because the danged horse would ride you to hell and back. He was not wrong. Dante keeps going long after other horses give up."

"Wonder what his secret is?" Abijah asked.

"This breed of horse is special. Called a California Vaquero. You have to treat them with respect. His old owner didn't know how to treat him, and that's why he bit. You have to ask them to do what you want, and they have to understand what you are training them to do. They do not take kindly to orders or rough handling."

"That makes sense to me, Brother. I always tell my team what I expect and thank them for their work. I think it makes all the difference. Pa taught us that, didn't he?"

"Yes, he sure did. And that's why Dante likes you, 'Bije. He knows he can trust you."

"Only, don't tell Pa about your horse's name. He doesn't josh around about hell, even if you got a ride back again," Abijah chuckled.

"You're probably right. I best get back to work now. I'm going to check the rest of the wagons. See you later, 'Bije."

"Don't worry about me. I'm alright, and I always like jawin' with you." Abijah waved his brother away.

The brothers met up that night with Parmenus and William Leffingwell. They discussed contingency plans, and Sandy had a copy of the route they were following and gave it to Darius, along with a list of route markers and instructions. The men stood on the edge of the campsite and kept their voices hushed so that nobody else would hear and become alarmed.

Abijah lay under the wagon that night and replayed the conversation in his head. When sleep claimed him, he dreamed of his brother's horse. In the dream, Dante and Abijah could speak to one another. The horse instructed him which way to ride, how far to travel, where he wanted to graze, and where to find the sweetest clover. He spoke of the best places for humans to hunt and fish, where the mountain lions waited, and where the rattlesnakes might strike. Then the war horse said to Abijah, "You're a good man, little brother, but you'll never ride me."

Abijah startled awake. He wondered if he should tell his brothers about the specter of Dante. He laughed at himself, not sure if the dream calmed him down or made him more confused.

Wednesday nights were campfire nights for the men-folk. They met up after dinner while the women put the children to bed. Any grievances from the trail were aired and, if possible, resolved. As usual there was a lot of concern about how hard Sandy pushed the group. He tried his best to remain patient, but it sometimes felt as though people were being purposely difficult.

He faced the men, implored them to grasp the importance of what he asked of them. "You'll thank me when we cross the Sierras before the snow comes. We cannot winter in the mountains without proper provisions. You know the horrific story of the Donner Party journey, and I refuse to let such a thing happen while I am the scout for this operation."

The group quieted as the harsh truths came out. There wasn't an adult on this venture who hadn't heard the story of the ill-fated pioneers. They worried they'd suffer the same—stranded in the snow, without food, one by one frozen to death, and finally, for the last desperate few—the unthinkable—cannibalism.

A man Sandy didn't recognize spoke up. "Sir, I'm James Cooper. We understand what you're saying, but we still have problems. Some people need help and won't ask for fear of appearing weak." His words captured the group's attention, and there was grumbled agreement.

"Thank you for speaking up, Mr. Cooper. I can't help folks if they don't tell me what's needed, but I do not abandon those I am responsible for." All the men shifted uncomfortably at his declaration. Their shame was palpable. "You tell me what's broken, and we'll work it out."

"Please listen to my son. He's an honorable man, and he will get us safely to California." Parmenus gave the group a stern look.

"My wife needs help somethin' awful. She's making herself sick, caring for the babies, and trying to help me with the animals." The man who spoke up was tall and thin and looked as though he was at the end of his tether. "My left front wheel is about to give up; I'm afraid to run it any further," said the next.

"My old horse lost a shoe, I've got another, but every time I try to put it on, the danged beast kicks me." The needs and complaints were many but everything was within their power to fix.

"Now we're getting somewhere. Let's work together. We're gonna get this sorted tonight—no shame in askin' for help when you need it. Our lives depend on each other." The mood was leveling out, and the spirit of cooperation was in the air.

"You there? Tell your wife to bring the little ones to our wagon tomorrow afternoon. They can stay for a while, and my sisters will mind them. Meantime, we'll see about helping you with your animals. Mister, we'll get your wheel fixed before we leave tomorrow. And you, with the pipe, my brother, Abijah, will shoe your horse. He's an accomplished farrier and an expert with ornery critters." That got a laugh, and someone in the crowd shouted 'four-legged or two-legged?' and every man left the warmth of the fire feeling more secure. A few waited around to discuss their problems privately, and as promised, Sandy stayed until everyone got the help they needed.

As father and son walked back to camp, they discussed the issues that had come to light. "Pa, until tonight, I didn't realize how poorly prepared some folks are. I assumed anyone signing up for the trail would be a bit more self-sufficient, but most of these men are as green as can be. We need to watch them closely, or they're not going to make it to California."

"I was afraid the crowd was going to turn on you, boy, but you got them sorted right," said Parmenus.

"Just trying to do the best I can. I know what to expect on this trail, but tonight I got lucky. What happens when they give me a problem I can't talk my way around?"

"The Lord provides, but you've gotta pray for guidance." Sandy shook his head but remained silent. He meant no disrespect, but there were times when he questioned his father's words and faith. Parmenus gave him a wink and walked back to camp.

Chapter Five
Fort Kearney, Nebraska to Fort Laramie, Wyoming

Marilla held onto the reins and watched as the miles rolled by. It was a day like all the other days on the trail—sore muscles and new vistas. She looked behind her and Martha was telling Samuel a story while working her way through a pile of mending.

"Spell me here, if you please. I need to check on Mary and Liza." The girls had been walking alongside the wagon, singing as they passed the time, but then Marilla got distracted watching clouds in the distance and when she looked back, the girls were gone. Perhaps they'd gone off trail to relieve themselves or spied wildflowers that wanted picking. Marilla started searching when she saw Mary running towards her.

It took a minute for the girl to catch her breath; her face was beet red. "I turned around for a minute, and Liza was gone. Mama, we've got to find her," Mary cried.

"Martha, we're going to search for Liza."

"I'll stay with the wagon and keep my eye on Sammy." Martha looked at her, and Marilla saw the fear in her eyes.

"We *will* find her." Marilla felt sick to her stomach. She followed Mary back towards the farm wagon to spread the terrible news.

"Have you seen Pa or Sandy?" Darius was at the reins and shook his head in disbelief.

"Pa's talking to the folks just behind us. Not sure where Sandy is. If I see him, I'll tell him you're looking. We need to pull off and stop until she's found," Darius looked around wildly, trying to see where his little sister might be. *Had she been kidnapped? Snake bit?* His imagination ran wild.

Marilla ran up to her son with his team of oxen. They were motionless for less than a moment before Sandy rode up to them and they'd delivered the frightening news.

Marilla felt a cold sweat on her back and shivered with worry. Every moment lost meant the possibility of Liza getting further from her family.

Sandy jumped from his horse. "Ma, here's Pa coming now. How far back do you think she disappeared?"

"I don't know. Half a mile or so? Mary said she got distracted for just a moment. And now Liza's vanished. I've got to find my little girl." Marilla hurried away, following Mary in the opposite direction the wagons were traveling. *"Liza, Liza!"* they cried until their voices were raw.

Between Sandy and Parmenus, the rest of the group got the news. Everyone who could be spared joined the search. The trail was a quarter of a mile or so from the river, and the search party fanned out to comb the sandy banks for some sign.

The hunt continued all afternoon. The child was gone without a trace. It was finally decided that they'd set up camp where they were, and hopefully, the girl would be reunited with her family the following day.

Parmenus found his wife standing at the river's edge, hand shading her eyes from the sun as it moved westward. He approached her, and she came into his arms, desperate for comfort. "Parmenus, I can't go on without her." Her eyes were rimmed with red, and tears had traced muddy tracks down her cheeks.

"We'll find her. God wouldn't let us come this far to lose our sweet Liza forever." Although his words comforted some, Marilla wondered what would happen if Liza couldn't be located by morning. She shivered in fear.

Her voice was low, defeated. "We can't expect the entire wagon train to wait for us. We are losing precious time. They'll have to move on without us."

"Don't think that way. Pray for her safety, pray for her return. That and keep the search going." But how long could they stay separated from the rest of the group?

Eventually, they stopped for the night. Darius brought Mary back to camp, and Martha got the girl fed and bedded down. Marilla refused sleep, she stayed up, keeping the fire going, and hoping that Liza might see the light and be guided through the dark.

The rest of the group was understandably uneasy and watchful in their camps. Mothers held fast to their children, frightened that they could be the next to disappear. The men kept watch, staring into the dark distance.

The Secret Lives of Ancestors

When morning arrived, and Liza still hadn't turned up, the other families set about the sad business of packing up to get back on the trail. Darius, Sandy, and Abijah rose before dawn to continue the search until the last moment when the rest of the Leffingwell group resumed their journey.

"I'm going, Parmenus. If she's hurt, I can tend to her. Stay with the family and keep them safe, Husband. Darius will come with me. We'll get her back, I promise."

"Borrow one of Leffingwell's horses and come back to me, Wife. Bring our daughter back safe." Parmenus and Marilla hugged.

Sandy gave them instructions about where they would find the group once they'd found Liza. He hugged his mother and brother and they prayed they'd be reunited within a day or two at the most.

"Ma, we'll find her. You'll see." Darius' confident words made a lie of his expression.

"I cannot give up. I have to find her."

With a last look at his wife, Parmenus held his hand up to his heart, said a somber goodbye, and hoisted himself up into the wagon. No matter the outcome, they couldn't jeopardize the rest of their group.

The travelers minus three moved on until the late afternoon, hoping to make up for the time they lost the day before. The wait was agonizing and everyone that had gone on ahead did so with heavy hearts.

Come midday, there was a change in the air; a thrum of energy that vibrated up through the soles of their feet—perhaps it was a sense shared by the collective. The news passed from wagon to wagon, all the way up to Parmenus. Liza was found alive. Everyone came to a halt. They waited in line for a few minutes until Sandy told everyone they were stopping for the night. They set up camp and waited anxiously for news.

"There they are. I see them!" exclaimed Mr. Leffingwell. Darius rode into camp, out of breath, his horse in a lather.

"It's Liza. She's alive, Pa, she's alive! Get a sack of flour from provisions."

Parmenus tried to comprehend. "Where's my daughter? Where's my Marilla?"

"They're coming, Pa. We gotta to trade for her. A Pawnee boy has her, and she's alive."

Understanding dawned and Parmenus grabbed the flour and rode with Darius to where his wife and daughter were waiting with a boy who looked to be about Abijah's age. The boy sat motionless on a beautiful spotted pony. His expression was closed and gave nothing away, but it was plain to see, he was too thin and shivering in the chill of the evening. Liza seemed unharmed and was now riding on the back of Marilla's horse, her arms clutched at her mother's waist and her eyes wide as she rested her cheek against the safety of Ma's back.

Parmenus rode up with the offering, which he presented to the boy. "Thank you for keeping my daughter safe." The boy nodded, turned his horse around, and rode away along the river before finally crossing.

Liza watched as he rode away, her hand raised in goodbye, but the boy didn't look back. Marilla and Liza rode slowly; they whispered to each other the whole way back. Darius and Parmenus rode in close protective formation as they returned to where the group had stopped for the night.

Folks looked up from their campfires as they rode by, calling out their hellos and good wishes. There would be time for explanations the next day, and the fear and stress on the entire group would ease overnight as everyone took their well-earned rest.

As Marilla and Liza approached, Martha jumped up from her place at the fire, where she'd kept food warm in anticipation of their return.

Mary was so relieved to see her sister back safely where she belonged; she wept with joy. Parmenus hugged his wife before leaving to help Abijah settle the animals for the night.

Marilla was worn out but grateful to have her daughter back. "Liza, sit with me while Martha gets our supper served."

"Yes, Mama."

Liza was filthy, had lost her bonnet somewhere along the way, and her arms and legs were covered in bloody scratches and bruises. Her mother slowly washed her cuts and cleaned the dirt off her face and hands.

"It stings, Mama."

"I know, just a little more. Need to clean out the dirt."

"I was frightened I'd never see you again." A few tears escaped, and Liza took in a deep quivering breath.

Marilla listened as her daughter told her about her experience. As far as she could tell, hunger, cold, and being scratched up were the worst things to happen to the girl.

Later when everyone was fast asleep, Parmenus lay next to his wife as she cried silently. Relief washed over her as her husband held her tight against his side.

Abijah watched intently as the landscape changed and he drove his oxen forward. He loved the sounds of the Platte River, the whooping cranes, the rushing waters, and the wind as it whipped through the grass. Every day was something new and thrilling. The further they traveled, the stronger and more sure of himself he became.

He heard Liza before he saw her running up to him. "Morning, Liza." He greeted. She smiled sweetly and held out what his mother had sent for him. She'd brought him a hunk of bacon rolled up in a flapjack and slathered with honey left from breakfast.

As soon as he'd eaten, Liza started her happy chatter. "Bije, do you think Blue is strong enough to get us to California?" She grabbed onto his free hand.

"Well, Blue's my b...b-best ox," Abijah said with pride. "He's the strongest of the team, and he'll take us wherever we want to go. Old Boy will follow what Blue does, and the others will follow the lead pair. They'll make it, don't you worry." She patted his arm and smiled at him.

"'Bije, I'm not afraid of Indians anymore."

Abijah was surprised she wanted to talk about her harrowing experience. "You were very brave, little Sister. But don't you ever run off like that again. We were all s...s-scared to death." He looked down at her face and squeezed her hand.

"I didn't run off. I just lost track of where I was. The Pawnee boy wrapped me up snug in his blanket. He saved me from freezing at night and wasn't mean at all. And he brought me back to you!"

"Did he understand English?"

"He talked to me, but when I didn't understand him, he gave up."

"Did he give you anything to eat?"

"He shared water with me and a little dried meat when we stopped for the night. He made a fire, and we sat close to each other to keep warm. I don't think he slept much because it was so cold, and I had his blanket. I shivered all night, but he was quiet as a mouse."

"You stay close to the wagon from now on. We've got too much traveling to do to spend time looking for lost children."

"I won't get lost again, 'Bije, I promise."

"I've got work to do and you've got chores." He winked at Liza and watched as she ran back to the wagon.

Over the miles, the wear and tear on the wagons was considerable. As Sandy rode up and down the line, he saw that some required repairs and called a halt for the afternoon. Everyone appreciated the opportunity to stay in one place a few extra hours.

Sandy watched as Darius checked the tarring on the bottom of their wagons. He was grateful and impressed by the younger man's diligence. "How's that holding up?"

"Hey, Brother. Pretty well, I'd say. Of course, we won't know until we cross deep water, but I was mighty careful when I painted it on before we left St. Jo. I'll check the wheels. As you're making your way down the line, if you see anyone else struggling, let them know I'm available to help out, alright?"

"I'll ask around and let you know." Based on what Sandy had seen, he knew Darius would be in demand. Knowing he could count on his brother to keep their wagons in order was a load off his mind. Big or small, if a thing was broken, Darius could most likely fix it.

"You've gotta keep me busy, keep me out of trouble." Darius' mouth lifted in a grin.

In addition to his skills, his younger brother had a way with people that he did not. Sandy was more reserved, taciturn, whereas Darius was affable; always had a kind word for folks. People felt comfortable enlisting his help when they needed it.

"You know what we need?" Darius had a twinkle in his eye and Sandy knew better than to give in too easily.

"I don't know, soft beds, full bellies, a good night's sleep?" He shot a smile back.

"That does sound nice, but I was thinkin' what we need is a little entertainment?" Darius' eyes were alight.

"What are you thinking?" Sandy was suspicious of anything that might divert attention from their travel West. They had to get to California ahead of heavy weather; no time for nonsense.

"Why can't we have a dance some night after dinner? There must be someone who could fiddle, or maybe just some singing around the campfire. Brother, it's gonna improve everyone's mood faster'n you could imagine." Darius got a sort of faraway look in his eyes and Sandy wondered who he was thinking about because he was sure that expression was caused by some young lady in the group.

"Stay up too late dancing and carrying on, and you'll be no good the next day along the trail. That's how folks get hurt."

"Now you sound like an old man. We won't let it go on too late, Sandy. Just a few songs and dances around the fire; it's what we need."

"I'll run it by Pa and Mr. Leffingwell. We'll see what they say." Darius was impossible to deny; always had been and it was the source of minor irritation when they were younger. Now, Sandy just found it interesting. He wouldn't be surprised if some day his brother ended up in politics.

"Aw, Brother, thank you!" Darius whistled while he finished greasing the supply wagon.

William Leffingwell got up to deliver the news at the Wednesday campfire meeting. "The first order of business tonight is the state of our provisions. It's early in our journey, but I want everyone to get into the habit of keeping track if you aren't already doing that. The head of each family should know what they are likely to run short of and what might be in excess." As expected, his announcement was met with a few grumbles. "Just don't want there to be any surprises, you understand."

"On to brighter topics. It has been brought to my attention that our group could use an evening of dancing and singing, and I think it's a fine idea. A few hours of entertainment is what our community needs. So, Saturday evening, we will hold our first-ever wagon train dance. Bring your sweethearts, your children, and your parents. We'll resume the trail as usual Sunday morning after worship. This dance is open to every member of our wagon train." The collective responded favorably with claps and whistles.

Within a few minutes, there were volunteers of fiddlers, and a storyteller that would make the evening a fine time.

When the meeting was over, Parmenus found Marilla for a few moments conversation before they turned in for the night.

"Can you do a little baking for a dance on Saturday?"

Marilla laughed. She'd known this was coming. "Eunice already mentioned it tonight at our ladies' gathering. I expected you'd ask me about those pies. Every family will contribute a little something."

"Of course, whatever you make will be the most delicious. Maybe we should have a contest to see who can make the best campfire pie," Parmenus teased.

"More like, which pie has the most scorch marks, or whose pie sticks worst to the kettle."

"Sandy told me Darius came up with the idea for this dance. Do you think that boy's looking for a sweetheart?"

"He's the right age, and there are eligible young ladies in our group."

Talking about children growing up always made Marilla a bit melancholy, made her feel the passage of time. Eventually, all of their children would grow up, get married, and leave the nest. Her eldest boy had already found his one true love, and Marilla thought that he and Cyndi Leffingwell made a wonderful couple. Darius, Martha, Mary, and Abijah probably wouldn't be far behind.

The girls all resembled Marilla—dark hair, eyes that went from silvery grey to pale blue, fair complexions, broad faces with high cheekbones and freckles, and strong bodies. The boys favored Parmenus, muscular physiques forged by daily labor, dark hair, generous smiles that reached up to flashing blue eyes, large, beak-like noses, and angular faces. Sandy and Darius were tall like their father and moved with a lumbering gait, while Abijah stood at just five feet, five inches. He was sinewy with muscles still under development, and although smaller than the older men in the family, he could easily work from before sunup to after sundown. Her children were graced with keen intelligence, beautiful singing voices, and sharp wit, and all could nearly talk a person to death. Even baby Samuel was a chatterbox.

The next evening, a few ladies came by to visit Marilla. They sat by the fire, knitting, or mending while the light was still good, but eventually everyone drifted back to their families. All but one woman.

"Is there something I can help you with, Priscilla?" Marilla looked at the woman in the firelight and saw utter exhaustion in her expression.

"I hope so. Only, please don't tell anyone, but I'm expecting again," she whispered.

Marilla noticed the dark circles under the other woman's eyes. "How are you feeling?"

"Well, at least now I know what was bothering me. I've been sick in the mornings and can't tolerate bouncing around in the wagon but walking seems to help."

"Not to worry, your secret is safe with me, lass. I've got just the thing. Make yourself a nice pot of tea with these herbs. Just a pinch at a time, and don't swallow the raspberry leaves; strain them out. No more than a cup a day." She rummaged in her herb basket and presented Priscilla with dried raspberry leaves and chamomile flowers. "How far along?"

"Not very, but I'm not ready for everyone to hear the news just yet. My husband guessed pretty quickly, but I don't want to tell the children. They'll never stop asking questions, and I am just too tired to answer."

Marilla laughed softly, "That is the way of it with the little ones. You send your children here if you need some rest. We'll watch them for you, Priscilla."

"You and your girls already helped me so many times, it shames me that I haven't repaid you."

Marilla gave Priscilla a gentle hug. "Don't be ashamed, we've very quickly become family, haven't we? I can help you and I'm happy for it. Whatever you might need, no repayment necessary."

The exhausted mother hugged Marilla hard and then walked wearily back to her camp.

Marilla and Parmenus watched as their children rushed off to the dance. The girls traded off minding Samuel so their parents could enjoy an evening. "Come on, Wife, let's not dawdle."

"There's no rush, Parmenus. We'll get there in good time." Earlier, her daughters had woven wildflower crowns for their hair and surprised Marilla with her own. She adjusted it over her brow and gave a handmade boutonniere to her husband for his lapel. Parmenus offered his arm, and they walked to where the dancers and musicians awaited them.

The soft voices and fiddle music rose in the air as the sun set on the day. "What a beautiful night. Feels special, doesn't it?" Marilla's eyes twinkled as she looked at her handsome husband.

"Magical, I'd say." Parmenus gathered her in his arms for their first dance together in so long; Marilla couldn't remember when the last one had been. She grinned with delight and pointed discreetly at some of the other dancers. The young people were shy with one another as they awkwardly made their way through the waltzes and reels. "Were we ever that young, do you think?" he asked, his voice low and soft in Marilla's ear.

"You know we were. Seems just like yesterday you were courting me, my love." She cradled his cheek with her hand and stood on her tiptoes to give him a kiss.

Martha waved to her parents; she looked content. "Mama, can you imagine wanting to dance after walking all day? But here we are, and having the best time." Before Marilla could answer, Martha drifted away, and the next time she saw her eldest daughter, she was dancing with an unfamiliar boy.

"Parmenus, do you know him?" The boy in question was doing his best to keep off Martha's toes to no avail; his face flushed with exertion and embarrassment. However, Martha was a patient partner, and the two eventually found their way around the dance floor, laughing as the song ended.

"Huh. I know I've met him, but I can't remember his name or who his people are for the life of me. Her brothers will keep the boy in order. No reason to worry."

"Oh, I'm not worried, just curious. It's wonderful to see all the happy faces here tonight." She sneaked another quick peck on her husband's cheek.

Abijah awoke with a smile as he remembered last evening's festivities. He took a moment to let the images and sounds of the dance play again in his mind before beginning his day. Dew had collected on his old quilt, and he could smell damp earth and grass. He heard movement close by and just as he was about to crawl out from under the wagon he was poked at.

"Get up, 'Bije." His older brother had come by to help him get ready for the day.

"I'm up, Darius, I'm up." Abijah yawned and stretched. "Gonna be a warm one today." Darius grunted in agreement, stirred the coals from the fire, and set the kettle on for tea.

A basin of water was left out for washing, and Abijah scrubbed his face and neck before beginning his morning's work.

"I'll bring your tea when it's ready." Abijah nodded his thanks, smashed an old hat down on his head, and left camp to relieve himself in the privacy of a stand of trees.

He'd finished up with Old Blue when Darius found him, cup in hand. "Take a moment, Brother. Here's a biscuit from last night."

"Thank you." He didn't linger over his morning brew but drank and ate as he looked after the team. "Let's check on the rest of the animals. I expect we'll be heading out soon after Sunday service." Darius fed the chickens as Abijah took the milk cow to graze. "I had a lot of fun last night. How about you?"

"Oh, yeah. Real good time. I saw you dancin', 'Bije."

"Did you see me take a turn with the Widow B..B-Barnes? She's a real good dancer," Abijah laughed, his eyes alight with humor.

"Yeah, and I saw you dancin' with Ma and little Liza, too."

Abijah raked up the mess the milk cow had made and dropped the patties into a bucket to dry for later use as a starter for the cook fire. "Did you see Sandy dancing with Cynthia? They make a nice couple." He looked over and watched his ma making breakfast, and Mary trying to get Samuel cleaned up. "Look at Sammy—he hasn't been awake more than a minute and is already covered in dirt."

"I guess we'll celebrate a wedding when we get settled in California," Darius predicted.

"That'd be nice. I tried to find a young lady, but they were already dancing with the other boys."

"I'm sorry about that, 'Bije." Darius was protective of his younger brother. He looked him up and down to make sure all was well.

"Don't be, Brother. I already know I'm going to meet my girl in California, and we're going to have a ranch, and we're going to raise milk cows and babies. I dreamt it."

"You sure have some interesting dreams." Darius' mouth quirked slightly, and he shook his head. "Last night I convinced Samantha Tyrell to dance with me. She's the pretty girl with long red hair."

"I know who she is. Maybe you'll m...m-marry her," Abijah teased.

Darius gave a little snort. "Definitely not. Her people don't seem too friendly, and I don't think they like our family much."

Abijah looked around and saw everyone beginning to gather. "Guess it's time for prayers. Let's get it over with so we can get back on the move." He put away the rake and the bucket and followed Darius and the rest of his family for their informal service.

Pa led the worship. Abijah didn't put much stock in religion, but he didn't begrudge others their faith. Most people seemed to find comfort in it, but he'd rather find his in nature.

Chapter Six

Fort Laramie, Wyoming
to Fort Hall, Idaho

Abijah looked all around. *I cannot believe this is where I find myself.* He couldn't get over the beauty of the skies across the prairie. One moment the sun beat down upon his back, and the next he felt the chill and watched as clouds shifted and turned an ominous blue-black that met the horizon with only a tiny sliver of light far off in the distance. The animals raised their heads and sniffed at the air; Abijah did the same. Rain was coming and he suspected it wouldn't be a gentle shower.

The group continued as long as they dared but the mud sucked them in and bogged everyone down. They plodded along until someone got stuck so bad they couldn't go any further without help. Men armed with picks, shovels, and tarps slogged through to the first family stuck in the mud. They freed the wagon and then moved onto the next.

Abijah joined his family and they ate a quick meal of leftover flapjacks and jerky. There was still one more family to extract from the mud, and they were anxious to get it done before darkness made it too hard to see.

Everyone cheered when the last wagon was worked free. "Mighty thankful for your help!" said the young man they'd assisted. His wife stood next to him with a baby in one arm and a little girl in the other.

Abijah took a handkerchief out of his back pocket and tried to wipe some of the dried mud off his face, but he ended up smearing it around even more.

The travelers reached the banks of the Platte River near where they'd be crossing in late afternoon. The day was mild, but as it grew later in the afternoon, the wind kicked up. The result was a sky of deep blues and purples, with pink and golden clouds.

As the sun set, mothers and older daughters set up camp and prepared the evening meal. It was decided that the men would try their luck at duck hunting. There was no real urgency to their supply of meat, but it was always best to catch or hunt what they could instead of depleting provisions. This night, their efforts were unsuccessful and they returned to camp quiet and empty-handed.

Darius was first back to camp and sat at the fire. Mary greeted him with a hot cup of tea. A few men trudged by and he waved at them in silent greeting. They were dispirited and he hated to leave things without a friendly word so he tried to bolster the mood. "We'll try again tomorrow at sunrise before we ford the Platte." After the last man passed by, Darius got his kit out and cleaned his shotgun.

Just before bed, Abijah sat at the river's edge, and tried to calm his jittery nerves. He took deep, calming breaths and allowed nature's music to bring him peace. He wished he could stay in this place for another day and learn more about the terrain and its wildlife.

The Platte was the largest body of water they'd traverse on the way to California. Their group had been following it for miles, keeping the river bank to their right. Although no longer swollen from winter's floods, the current was still swift. Getting to the other side wasn't without danger, and the mood in camp was alive with excitement. The Leffingwell party joined other travelers and in all, fifty wagons, along with livestock and people, would make the crossing in the morning.

Campfires were aglow in the darkness, and the murmuring of voices carried on the breeze. Crossing the Platte was a major milestone in their journey and the excitement was palpable. Everyone's nerves jangled and filled their exhausted minds with unsettling dreams.

As promised, Darius and a group of men went out early to try to increase their stores of meat. The hunt yielded enough ducks for each family. The pintails were beautiful auburn-headed creatures and provided a good amount of meat, rich in protein and fat, and a welcome change in their basic diets.

While the hunters were out, Sandy surveyed the river to ensure they'd be crossing at the best spot. He trusted the Mormons who ran the barge operation, but as he was responsible for the group, he felt it was his duty to double-check for safe conditions. He'd met these same men when he passed through on his way back home from the war. Yesterday, they'd recognized him and greeted him with handshakes and smiles. Today though, they were all business with watchful expressions.

"Our group's crossing first, and your family will lead the way," Mr. Leffingwell confided in Sandy.

Sandy looked towards the river. "Good to get it over with, I suppose." The fees had already been paid, and the barge was ready to load up for the first crossing. So far, there had been no bickering between his group and the Mormon men who owned the operation. It was a flat fee of five dollars per wagon, and anything else was negotiated separately.

He said a little prayer that luck and weather would hold and approached the line of wagons. Sandy watched as everyone tied down their loads. They checked their precious cargo and barrels of provisions one last time.

When he was satisfied his group was ready, Sandy worked with his pa and brothers to get their wagons loaded onto the barge. Darius tucked extra oilcloth around the flour and animal feed sacks and wished they had more barrels for their supplies.

"Ma," began Sandy, "You, Martha and Mary, and the little ones are going to cross on the barge with our wagons. Pa, Darius, and Abijah will take the larger animals; they'll swim them across. I got some trunks and barrels wedged in the back of the wagon, and you can sit on those. It's going to be okay, Ma. I promise."

Darius joined him and his mother and gave her a reassuring hug. "We'll make it. Sandy knows what he's doing."

"I trust you boys and your father. We better get started. I can already imagine us on the other side." Sandy watched his mother straighten her shoulders as she seemed to draw courage to herself. He never ceased to be amazed by her strength, even when he knew she was doing something that scared her.

As the barge made its way across the Platte, Abijah got himself ready to swim across with his animals. He'd been up since before sunrise. He was nervous and wanted to ensure everything was ready to go and went over the plans in his head while he worked. Sandy would cross just ahead on horseback, swimming when the water became too deep. Once they'd made it to the other side, he'd help Darius,

Abijah, and his pa with the rest of the livestock. It was dangerous, and there were many stories of men and animals drowning, but Abijah tried not to think about his fears.

"How d...d-deep do you think it is in the middle? How strong is the c...c-current?" In times of stress, the boy's stutter became more pronounced—he was feeling the pressure. There were so many things that could go wrong, and Abijah hoped he'd have the strength he needed to lead his animals.

"Stop fretting, boy. The team will feel your fear. Let the Good Lord guide you. Sandy says this is the best spot for us to cross, and you will make it with those oxen." Abijah nodded, and his pa left him beside the river pondering the job ahead.

He stood with Blue and Old Boy and the rest of the team, reassuring them and tightening the leads. They grunted and snorted, and he felt them quivering and twitching, and then moving forward, just as he'd trained them.

"Well, Blue, guess we better get after it."

With no time for him to panic about the job ahead, Abijah closed his eyes a moment and took a deep breath. He felt the sun warm on his back and the breeze whispering on his skin, raising gooseflesh. No more stalling; the sooner he started, the sooner he could finish. He opened his eyes, and there was Sandy, giving him the "come along" wave.

"Head up, Blue. Head up, Old Boy. Get up." Abijah's commands were smooth and confident. Once the front pair started, the other six moved along. He had total control as he led them down the muddy banks and into the rushing current.

He gave a little yelp when the river bottom dropped off, and he went from knee-deep to up to his hips in the icy water. "Damn, but that's cold," he proclaimed. There was no time for uncertainty.

The crossing was the most dangerous thing he'd ever attempted, but the animals obeyed him, and he guided them well. At the deepest, Abijah hung on to the middle of the bow yoke on Blue and Old Boy. The water rose higher with each step forward until his feet no longer found purchase—his head went under the roiling depths, again and again, each time to come back up, gasping for air, choking on the Platte River. Blue was undeterred by the current, which settled the boy's nerves. His animals kept pushing forward. Finally, his feet found the solid ground on the river bottom. They'd made it through the deepest part.

"Blue! Old Boy! Get up! Get up!" Abijah coughed up water, and his loyal beasts spluttered and snorted for the rest of the crossing.

Abijah checked the animals' hooves when his father came over to see how he'd fared. "Let me help get 'em fed." Pa began to divide the feed.

"Thanks!" Abijah was still shaking with cold but he grinned from ear to ear. "Whelp, we did it. Got us across."

"We sure did." Pa crooned softly in Old Boy's ear.

Abijah brushed the mud off Blue's flank. The animal snorted once, but didn't seem bothered by the fact that it was saturated with river mud. "We lose any animals?"

"No, we didn't, but other folks did. One fellow lost two of his cattle, and Leffingwell lost a horse."

Abijah's happiness dimmed when he heard about the animals that had been taken by the river. "That hurts. I'm sorry for them."

"Come, Boss. Come, Boss!" Pa called the oxen. He was nearly as fond of those big old beasts as his son was. "I knew you'd make it safe across, Son. You did some good work, and you should be proud of yourself. Sandy's got the fire going already. Time for us to take our ease and warm our bones."

"I will, Pa. Just gonna finish up here, turn 'em out to graze, then I'll rest." His pa patted him on the shoulder.

"Don't keep your mother waiting too long, Son."

"I expect we're having duck tonight, huh?" The moment Abijah mentioned food, his stomach rumbled in agreement and he laughed. Pa had already started back to camp.

The oxen behaved just as Abijah had hoped they would. He would remember this day for the rest of his life and tell stories to his children, grandchildren and great-grandchildren. And everyone would know and be proud of his deeds. With these thoughts going through his mind, he couldn't help but smile and know he'd done his family proud.

Chapter Seven
Fort Hall, Idaho to California

The heat and the wind stripped away neighborly patience. Arguments broke out over petty grievances, and Sandy broke up fights when the otherwise reasonable men came to blows. Mothers who needed a good night's rest lost their tempers with the little ones. The children were listless, crying from empty stomachs, heat, and constant movement.

Food supplies were running low and because of this, there was plenty of room in the back of their wagons for everyone to sleep at night. Nobody said so outright, but it was obvious that some of the barrels were already empty. There were still enough oats for porridge and enough tea for a hot morning brew. The sugar, flour, and beans would just about make it to Sacramento if they were careful and lucky. And there was still hardtack and jerked beef. At night they set snares, hoping to lure a jack rabbit.

"Mary, can't we stop and rest? I'm so tired of moving. And I'm hungry. It's been so long since breakfast," Liza complained.

While Liza played with her rag doll, Mary helped Martha darn socks. Letting down hems, patching holes, and mending seams—the sewing and knitting would never end. Unfortunately, there wasn't money for anything new, but maybe there would be once they'd settled in California.

Mary let out a big sigh, thinking of all the things she wished might happen. She was sure Martha would marry soon, then maybe she'd find a young man of her own. After all, she was 18, and most girls her age already had husbands and children. "Martha, we've gotta find you a husband. Then it'll be my turn," she mused and giggled to herself.

From the front of the wagon, Martha turned around and gave her a funny look. "What are you talking about?"

Mary started, unaware that she'd said anything aloud. "Oh, just dreaming about California, that's all."

A few moments later, Liza broke in. "Mary, I'm hungry. Can we eat?"

"Alright, let me see what we have," Mary peeked in the basket, corn cakes smeared with honey. She broke off pieces for Liza and herself. Then she scrambled over the crates and poked her head out of the front of the wagon. Darius was driving, and Sister Martha sat next to him. Samuel was drowsing between them, quiet for once.

"Who wants some?" she asked.

Samuel woke with a sleepy smile at the mention of food. "I do, Mary, I'm hungry."

"Thank you, Sister," said Martha.

"I hope you enjoy it. When Ma gave me the basket this morning, she told me this was the last of the cornmeal." Mary gave Martha and Darius a knowing look and could see they, too, were worried about the dwindling provisions.

"I used the last of the cornmeal this morning, Parmenus." Marilla climbed down from the wagon to walk along with her husband.

He squinted down at her, the sun was blistering today. "And it was delicious. But what else have we run out of?"

"Time for us to take stock again, don't you think?" Marilla always felt better when she could share her feelings with her husband. It lessened the burden. "I knew we'd run through our supplies, but it feels mighty uncomfortable."

"Then we'd better go through every last bundle." He put his arm around her waist and drew her closer to him for a moment.

"Thank you." They walked along in silence for a while. Each kept the council of their own thoughts.

"How do you feel, Marilla? I know you must be tired, but you look well." He gazed upon his wife with an appraising eye.

"I feel well. I'll be grateful to reach our destination, but I have enjoyed our grand adventure so far." She stopped and tried to get some control over her windswept hair. "This land is surely beautiful—sometimes lush, sometimes stark, and I awaken each morning wondering what the day will bring. I've thought about what our lives will be like in California. I'm filled with hope."

Parmenus bent down and picked a wildflower and presented it to his wife. "I'm excited, too. Can't wait to get our new lives started.

This flower the same blue as your eyes," he said and tucked it behind her ear.

"Thank you, Husband," she said with a smile.

For the first time since their journey began, Parmenus felt prickling fear clawing at the back of his neck. His head pivoted on his neck searching desperately for a sign of life, of water, of salvation. He searched for answers. *Just keep moving*, echoed in his head. "Lord, help us make it to California," he prayed aloud. Surely, God heard his prayers.

They'd resupplied water back at Fort Hall but the desert heat parched throats. Parmenus picked up a smooth stone, wiped it off on the leg of his trousers and popped it into his mouth to suck on. He continued his walking vigil, determined his faith would not waver—unsure of what he hoped to find in the distance on that hard-packed trail.

Sandy approached his father on foot, his boots kicking up dust. "You've been up here on your own all day, Pa. Everything alright?" He offered his canteen.

"I'm fine, Son." He shook his head at the offer of Sandy's canteen.

Sandy didn't reply but took a short, unsatisfying swig of warm water.

"I needed the solitude, I expect," Parmenus said with a long sigh. "Reflection does me good in trying times."

Sandy cocked his head, and Parmenus could feel his gaze, feel his son assessing. "This part's the hardest, but we'll make it to the mountains before we run out of water, Pa." Now he looked back at his son, seeing the weariness on his face, the weight of responsibility on his shoulders, and nodded.

"I believe you." What else was there to say? Either they'd make it, or they wouldn't. But he tried to sound more confident than he felt. "I trust you, Son."

Sandy pulled off his ragged hat that he'd had since before he went away to war and ran his fingers through greasy hair. "Thank you. Couldn't we all use a bath, a bed, a chicken dinner, and some of Ma's berry cobbler?"

"That would be like heaven." Parmenus chuckled quietly. They walked along, mostly silent until it was time to make camp for the night.

Abijah lost one of his oxen two weeks out of Fort Hall and felt some guilt he was relieved it wasn't Blue or Old Boy. "Poor thing. He worked himself to death for us, Pa. Hate the thought of butchering him."

"Understand how you feel, but to waste that meat is a sin. Hard as it is, we need the sustenance." Pa was right. "I'll lead the remaining team while you take care of it. They're your animals—you do right by them."

"I'll do it. I'm not sure I can manage to eat it when Ma makes dinner tonight."

Abijah had watched as the poor beast's legs buckled. Finally, it dropped, collapsing in the dirt, and that was it. After his pa left him, he cut it up where it laid in the wagon tracks, tears streaming down his face. The other wagons passed by silently while Abijah performed his awful task. He just managed to keep his food in him.

That night Marilla made a stew with the meat and shared it with the whole camp. Everyone, including Abijah, ate their fill and thanked the poor beast. Two days later, the other yellow ox of the pair succumbed, and it was the same dismal process all over again. Other families had lost several mules; God knew the ox made a better meal.

They had to have fuel for the cook fires, and trees were in short supply, so dried dung was collected to burn. When that was used up, families burned barrels, supply crates, and eventually, what was left of the furniture. Grandpa's rocking chair, and Mother's carved wedding chest, all of it was sacrificed to the cause. It seemed an unending cycle—just when they thought they'd given their all, the pioneers were forced again to lighten their loads. Silverware, bone china, and fine tea-sets that had survived the arduous journey from England generations before were abandoned and the women cried helpless tears of frustration.

Feeling the need to witness what had been surrendered to the cause of survival, Sandy rode to the back of the wagon train and looked at a lifetime of possessions abandoned in the dusty traces. He recognized some of his own family treasures and felt wet tears on his cheeks. Ma must be heartbroken.

Sandy walked back to the end of the wagon train to see his sweetheart, Cynthia, and her parents. William Leffingwell sat in front at the reins; his wife, Eunice, was next to him, her head resting on his shoulder. Cynthia walked along beside them, quietly singing "Shenandoah." Her voice was nearly a whisper and sounded sad and sweet.

"Good morning, Mr. Leffingwell, Missus. Good morning, Cyndi." The older couple nodded and smiled down at him.

"Where's your horse, Sandy?" asked Mr. Leffingwell.

"He's hitched to the back of Pa's wagon, Sir. I'm trying to save his strength for the mountains. I'm a walking man now."

Leffingwell nodded. The poor man looked like he had the weight of the world on his shoulders.

His wife sat there with her head lolling on his shoulder. She whispered, "I thought perhaps he'd perished along with our horse."

"It could happen, but I hope it won't. I've had my horse, Dante, for a long time and we've been through a lot together."

"Sandy, how's your mama?" she asked.

"Ma's fine, tired of this desert, like the rest of us. Come by for a visit soon or shall I have her come to you?"

"That'd be real nice." Sandy looked at the older woman, her sun-bonnet was pushed back, and her thin grey hair hung down her back in a long braid. His ma and her had become close on this journey. "You tell her I said hello, and I look forward to sharing a campfire with her soon."

"I will, Ma'am."

"Walk with me for a while, Sandy?" Cynthia stepped a little closer to him.

Sandy tipped his hat. "I'd be pleased to."

There was just barely a hint of a breeze, and the sweat ran down Sandy's back . He wiped at his forehead with his kerchief every few minutes. Cynthia's bonnet was so large that her face was nearly covered. Sandy could just about see her if she tilted her head to the side and he leaned in close.

"You have a mighty nice singing voice. Would you sing some more while we walk?" Cyndi needed cheering up, he could tell.

"One more, and that's it. It makes me so thirsty." She took a dainty sip from her pa's water skin before starting.

She began in her soft, sweet voice - *Oh, do you remember Sweet Betsy from Pike? Crossed the wide mountain with her lover Ike ...*

When she finished her song, they continued without speaking for a while. They were companionable together, and he enjoyed spending time with her. His shoulder brushed up against hers. "Hold my hand, Cyndi?" She didn't answer but took his hand in hers.

"Do you think we have enough food to make it to California?" she asked him hesitantly.

"We'll be alright. Just have to be careful." As they walked along, Sandy tried to sound encouraging but he didn't want to outright lie.

Their situation was serious, but they'd get along if everyone cooperated.

Cyndi took a long exhale, "We had the last of the tea this morning." She looked into the distance and shook her head. "Are we ever going to get there, Sandy?"

"We'll get there. And Cyndi, my Ma's got tea, plenty of herbs should you and your mama need them, and she'll happily share with you."

"I wish we were back at the Snake River. I'd sit on the bank and put my feet in the cool water. It would be refreshing and clear and so nice to rest."

He gave her hand a little squeeze. She tilted her head, and he saw a little smile lift the corner of her mouth.

The Sierra Nevada Mountains rose majestically before the pioneers. Tomorrow would begin the upward trail into the mountains. Sandy walked his horse down the line of wagons, doing his regular afternoon check of the group. Generally, this was the time for friendly visits, questions, and a bit of joshing. But, today was different, and he could tell there was to be no more travel.

A man in a battered hat stopped his wagon, hopped down, and stood directly in Dante's path. Dante stopped with a snort. It was James Cooper, a man Sandy had come to think of as a friend. "What's happened, James? Everyone alright?"

"We 'bout ready to stop for today?" he asked softly as he swayed on his feet, bone tired. "My children can't go any further without a good meal and a good night's sleep. My wife is ready to drop in her tracks. I'm begging, you've got to let us stop for the night." His family, like the others, had reached their limit of hungry, thirsty, and too much sun. His lips were chapped, his eyes sunken, his face sunburned and yet pale from dehydration.

Sandy reached out and put his hand on the man's arm to steady him. "Everyone's done in. We're all stopping for the night."

Gratitude washed over James' face. "Thank you, Sandy." Then, as much as he'd like to stay and make sure his friend would be alright, Sandy left him standing on the trail and moved along to the next family.

It was that way at every wagon. People were relieved and thankful when Sandy brought the news. "Folks, we're pulling off the trail for the day. After supper, we'll share a campfire and a hot drink. Get yourselves a good rest because tomorrow begins our trek into the mountains, where God willing, we'll find fresh water and good hunting."

Coyotes howled in the distance. Abijah and his older brothers slept under the wagons, rifles at the ready to protect the remaining livestock from hungry predators. They spoke in whispers about the day and how tomorrow might unfold. It was their first night after the desert, and they'd begun their ascent into the Sierras. Relief was palpable.

"I'm so glad to be away from that damned desert." Abijah lay on his back motionless as he waited for the weariness of the day to claim him.

"Agree," said Darius. No matter how tired he was, evening time with his brothers was the time he liked most. The three brothers differed in personality, but they got along better than anyone he knew and had a deep respect for one another.

"Better grazing for the animals in the next day or so, I'd wager, we've got fresh water coming up, and we can hunt," Sandy said with quiet optimism.

"Everything smells fresh except us. We stink somethin' awful," Darius chuckled. "I'd give about anything for a bath or even a cold dunk in a river."

Abijah sighed. "I think the stars are brighter here, don't you?"

"Not much in the way of livestock left," observed Sandy.

Their talk had come down to drowsy observances. Darius realized at least three separate conversations were happening at the same time. "Nope, but that's the way of things, isn't it?"

"You're right, Dari. That's the way of things." Abijah rolled to his side, signaling his need for sleep. "Night, boys."

"Goodnight," said Darius.

"Time for sleep. Morning will be here soon enough." Sandy was snoring just moments later.

Abijah felt the hole that had been threatening in his boot finally give way. The sole on the other one was ready to break through, too. New footwear would have to wait, but maybe Ma had something he could stuff in the toe to make it last a bit longer. Regardless, he'd wait for the next stop to make repairs.

Their party limped along higher and higher up the eastern side of the Sierras. Rutted tracks gave way to red earth punctuated with massive slabs of granite and stands of cedar, pine, and fir trees. Progress came to a standstill when wheels needed repairs, which happened frequently. Then the zigzagging path up the mountain resumed.

Would they ever reach the crest? Abijah wondered as he drew in a deep breath, and the scent of pine filled his lungs. He craned his neck back and took a moment to stretch sore back muscles. Overhead he spied a buzzard searching for carrion.

Just ahead, Sandy's horse stopped picking his way forward.

"Hold up, Blue. Whoa, Old Boy." Abijah could see the trail petered out at the base of a nearly vertical rock face.

"Can't go around. Gotta go up," Sandy announced.

"Is there any other way?" Abijah looked up to where his brother pointed. It seemed near impossible.

"Maybe. Just need to make sure." Sandy tied his horse to a nearby manzanita shrub just off the trail in the shade and disappeared for a moment into the dense scrub. After a few moments, Abijah saw movement and heard his brother shouting. By the time Sandy came back, Pa and Darius had come ahead to see what was going on.

"Found us a deer trail." Sandy crashed through the thick underbrush. "It's going to take some doing, but we can make it up the mountain."

Most of the party and what was left of the livestock clambered up the steep, narrow trail to the top of the cliff. Parmenus devised a pulley system that would haul the wagons up the rock face once they'd been taken apart. His experience as a builder was exactly what was needed for him to rig the block and tackle. Once at the top, a group of men reassembled the prairie schooners.

Abijah stayed down below with a few other men to help guide the pieces up. They held the loose ends of the ropes so that nothing would bang and possibly shatter against the rocky face. Finally, the last pieces were hauled up, and the others climbed the steep trail to the top to meet their awaiting families.

Abijah was now the last man left at the base of the cliff. He looked up to where he needed to go and felt his heart beat like a drum in his chest. He crawled into the rope sling and held tight to the thick, greasy hemp.

There had been some argument with Darius earlier, "I'll be the last one up, Dari. I wanna feel what it's like to fly and really be free. Come on, Brother, you gotta let me do it." Darius had said all the right things about safety and recklessness, but in the end, Abijah got his way.

"Hot damn! Pull me up!" he hollered at the top of his lungs and gave the rope a yank. The rope jerked, and up he started. Abijah couldn't see Darius or anyone else, but he trusted his brother was up there, pulling him to safety.

His vantage was spectacular, and Abijah took in the views. The blue sky, the curious trees that grew right out of the cliff, the soaring eagles. As he rose higher, the sling began to arc back and forth. He made the mistake of looking down and felt the rush and tingle of vertigo.

"Help me!" he cried, but the wind stole his words. He banged painfully up against the rock face scraping hard against his hip and shoulder. The pain was sharp and startled him. He looked up and was hit by a small cascade of pebbles, dust, and a few larger rocks that had come loose.

Moments later, it was over and Abijah heard Pa, Sandy, and Darius—yelling as they pulled him over the edge. They plucked him out of the makeshift harness, and he couldn't wipe the grin off his face no matter how hard he tried. "You made it!" Darius clapped him on the back and held on to him as he stumbled a few steps.

By the time the wagons were put back together, it was too late to move on. The pioneers were more than happy to call it a night. Abijah cared for their few remaining animals and then got himself cleaned up. He scrubbed at his face, hands, and arms, trying to get the axel grease washed away. He realized it wasn't coming off until he could take a proper bath. *Worth the trouble,* he thought.

Darius called out to him. "Take your ease, Brother."

"No, 'Bije, horsey, horsey," begged Samuel.

Although exhausted by the day's adventures, he lifted the little boy onto his shoulders and galloped around the campsite. They galloped over to where his mother was cooking, and Samuel clapped his hands and squealed with delight.

"Abijah, put your brother down and come to supper!" exclaimed Marilla.

They woke up before dawn to thunder that vibrated the ground and the crack of lightning. "That was real close." Abijah got up quickly as water seeped into his bedroll and clothing. Darius was already up trying to move his soggy belongings to the shelter of the covered wagon. Another crack sounded, and a sugar pine 100 yards from where they'd slept took the hit. Samuel was crying; the sounds had scared him.

Ma handed Samuel down from the wagon bed into his father's waiting arms. The little boy's face was streaked with tears, and he buried his face in Pa's chest, trying to escape the booms and flashes of light.

"You're safe, Sammy. It's okay." Parmenus crooned and hugged him tight to his chest. "The storm will pass."

Sandy appeared, his normally calm demeanor absent. "Pa, take the family and find safety away from all these trees." He pointed to a spot about a quarter of a mile away. "Down in that little valley. You've got to get them out of here. Just the family—leave everything else up here along the trail. I'll meet you as soon as I've warned everyone else."

"Be careful, Son." Sandy exchanged a worried glance with his father. Parmenus gathered his family and began the trudge down to where his boy had indicated.

It took a while before everyone reached the valley to wait out the storm, but they all made it safely. Their waiting spot was more of a gradually sloping ravine than a valley, but it would suffice. It had to. This wasn't the first big storm the pioneers had weathered.

There was another strike of lightning, and in spite of the rain, the tree that was hit earlier caught fire. Eventually, the rain let up some, but the mud was causing run-off that rushed down the hill. The fire gained momentum and spread to nearby trees. The pioneers were in a dangerous predicament. All they could do was stay put and wait out the thunder and lightning and pray the spreading fire didn't engulf their abandoned campsite and the animals they'd left tied up. It was risky to remain so exposed and immobile, but they could do nothing else.

After another hour, the oppressive grey clouds cracked apart as the storm blew over. The mud was still a considerable deterrent, but at least the sun was out. It was safe enough to get everyone up the hill and back to their wagons.

They spent the rest of the day digging out, drying off, and checking on animals. Tomorrow they'd get back on the trail. The evening meal was hard-tack and jerky. The surge of adrenaline had now dissipated—their weariness was bone deep. There were a few whispered 'goodnights' then silence as they drifted off to sleep.

Mary and Liza had been sent out to gather herbs and berries, and the girls loved these treasure hunts. The day was warm, overcast with high clouds and Marilla was alone with her thoughts as she drove the big wagon. As she bumped along, she thought about her mama and wondered how she was faring. As soon as they reached their destination, she'd write to her and tell her all of their adventures. Marilla was anxious to get her family settled in California and tried to imagine living near the ocean.

Sandy had described the land where they would soon call home —the hills and mountains, the cold blue Pacific, the rocky shoreline, the smell of salt air and damp earth. Marilla imagined things would be very different from life in Missouri or at least she prayed it would be different. *I will not miss our leaky roof or the rotting timbers in the barn —the terrible humidity in summer and the ice and snow in winter. Undoubtedly, California will be a better life.* The closer they came to their new home, the more Marilla allowed herself to be caught up in the excitement.

Too soon, though, the girls begged for her attention. "Look at this, Ma," they called out.

"What is it, girls?"

"We found something pretty, but it smells strange and it's sticky. Is this a good plant, Mama?" From the pocket of her apron, Mary produced a dark green, feathery-leafed plant and handed it to her mother.

Marilla examined the plant, and thought back to her discussions with her son about the native plant life they'd encounter along the way. She sniffed at it, crushed a bit of the stem in her fingers, and sniffed again.

"I believe this is mountain misery," Marilla said with a smile. "A strange smell, but still lovely, I think."

The girls wrinkled their noses in distaste.

According to Sandy, the Indians in this area brewed it into tea and used it for treating lung ailments. Marilla hoped to meet some of the Miwok women who lived in this area's tribal lands. She was sure, if given the opportunity, she could learn about their plant medicines and perhaps she could trade some of her own knowledge, too.

"Please collect some for me. Don't take all of it; leave some for others."

As they traveled West, the Sierras gave way to the foothills. Thanks to Sandy's leadership and good fortune, the Leffingwell party made it through before the weather turned on them. Although they ached for their journey to end, a kind of giddiness overcame even the group's grouchiest. The golden grasses shivered in the wind, and enormous black oak trees dotted the rolling hills. Nights and mornings chilled the bones, but daytime was mostly warm sun on their backs and the unmistakable feeling of fall in the air.

For the first time since crossing the Platte, they encountered large groups of travelers not too far ahead or passing by in the opposite direction. Men on horseback, families in wagons and on foot, Wells Fargo stagecoaches—carrying passengers and perhaps gold. They crossed paths with military men in uniforms, miners, and other pioneers. After so many months of little contact with others, it was astonishing to be in the presence of so many strangers.

Many who passed greeted them with a cautious wave, but their warm hellos were usually met with suspicious glances. Sandy walked beside Abijah and their remaining oxen. "Not the friendliest folks I've encountered," Abijah observed.

"It's common for people on their way to the gold fields. Don't take it personal." Sandy had seen this behavior often when he traveled through California during and after the war. It was a symptom of gold fever. People were suspicious and kept their business to themselves.

Abijah wiped the sweat from the back of his neck with an old bandana. "You think they're carrying gold nuggets?"

"Might be. Wouldn't do to ask, though." Sandy chuckled.

"Think there are bandits hereabouts?" Abijah looked around, seeing danger in every shadow.

"Who knows, Brother, always good to keep your eyes open," he warned quietly. "They're known to travel these parts. And they'll kill you if you so much as look at them wrong."

It was September 23, 1853, and Sutter's Fort loomed in the distance. Now, nothing more than an abandoned ghost town, Parmenus wasn't sure what he'd expected, but he hoped the city of Sacramento offered more hospitality and supplies. Marilla sat next to him in the covered wagon, and they chatted about what supplies they needed to finish their journey to Petaluma.

"We look a fright, Parmenus. I hate meeting society without having a bath first." Marilla might joke about it, but he knew his wife was ashamed to appear so bedraggled in public.

"Anyone else who's come as far as we've come is going to look about the same. It won't be long before we replace our worn clothing, we'll have a proper bath and a good meal, perhaps get you a new bonnet. What do you say to that, Wife?"

"This may be true, but our shoes are worn through at the soles. I'm willing to wait until we reach our destination if you think it's best, but we look like beggars. I can only mend so much damage."

The Secret Lives of Ancestors

He patted her knee, and she leaned into him, resting her head on his shoulder.

"Still have a few pelts to trade. We'll see what we can get for those. We need feed for the animals and us as well. Nothing fancy, maybe some bacon and beans, coffee, tea, cornmeal. I expect high prices here, so I hate to buy much until we arrive in Petaluma."

"I can help too, Parmenus. I have herbs I can trade or sell." Marilla was determined to at least purchase wool for new stockings and socks for her family. What they had was in deplorable condition. More holes than stockings left. It would be a good project for the rest of their travel time and something Martha, Mary, and Liza could help with. And she'd be fibbing if she said she didn't want new bonnets for the girls and herself, and perhaps new shirts for her men.

"Do what you can, Wife. I'm sure you'll find ladies willing to trade while you visit. We'll make out just fine, you'll see. Sandy, Darius, and Abijah can help me negotiate for what we need. You'll stay with the wagons for now?"

"Of course," Marilla agreed.

"You'll have a chance later to go by the shops, I promise." Parmenus found a good place near the river with plenty of shade. Marilla and her daughters could keep an eye on Samuel as he ran around chasing ducks. He'd been in the wagon too long and had a lot of energy to burn.

The other families in their party ended up close by, and the women gathered to watch an endless parade of young boys and men unloading barges. They hauled sacks on their backs, rolled barrels, or pushed wheelbarrows with cargo bound for the shops along the dusty street.

"Look at all the burned-out homes and shops. Fire came through here recently, but they're already rebuilding." Martha sat in the open bed of the farm wagon and braided Mary's hair while Liza played quietly with Samuel. Every so often, one of the young men would pause his deliveries to tip his hat to Martha and Mary and utter a shy, "Good afternoon, ladies." The girls smiled sweetly and nodded their heads.

"I'm glad we won't be settling here, but still, it's interesting to watch all the different people. Have you ever seen so many foreign faces or heard so many different ways of speaking?" Marilla carefully separated her bundles of herbs and wrapped them in individual packets. "Martha, will you take Mary around to tell people I'd like to trade my herbs? Find out what they might have in exchange."

"I will, Ma. Let me take a look to see what you've got." Martha peered in the basket—lavender, comfrey, chamomile, witch hazel, feverfew, golden seal, bay leaf, and a few bundles of the mountain misery. "We'll bring back some customers."

There was quite a demand for Marilla's herbs, and she and Liza spent the afternoon rolling little cones of paper filled with different blends. Some came with coins, and others came with supplies to trade.

Sacramento was loud. Everywhere raised voices, boots stomping on the wooden boardwalks, the slamming doors. And it stunk. It was not clean like the mountains or the arid scent of sage in the desert. It smelled of too many bodies in close proximity, horses and cows, and the smoky fires of a blacksmith forge. "When do we get out of here, Sandy?" Abijah was anxious to get back on the trail and away from the chaos. Although he wasn't sure exactly where it might be, he could not wait to find his way home.

Sandy's brows knit as he looked at Abijah. At first he thought maybe his younger brother was joking, but on second glance, he could see the discomfort. "Come on, now, we just arrived. Let's walk around and see what we can find."

Abijah and Sandy walked the streets of Sacramento, taking in all the new sights and sounds. Access to the river wasn't far from the shops and there were saloons, a mercantile, a milliner, a stable, a dentist and doctor's office, and a hotel. They saw men and women who strolled about in fancy clothes, hats, and bonnets, and others who looked about as trail worn as their own family. There were children with dirty faces running barefoot by the river and ladies traveling in grand carriages. It was fascinating, but Abijah was more interested in the busy waterway and getting to know the town than he was in meeting new folks. "Wonder how it is in the rain?"

Sandy pointed at the watermarks on the buildings and the trees nearby. "It floods regular. Must make it hard for the merchants."

He looked back towards their wagons and caught a glimpse of his sisters. Sandy hoped they'd be able to walk around to the shops later. It wasn't fair that they had miss out on the fun.

The scent of roasting meat caught Abijah's attention and he sniffed at the air, trying to identify the source. "Aren't you about starving, Sandy? If we were still on the trail, I'd be fine, but the smell of that meat is about to do me in."

"I know it. My stomach's growling fierce. Let's find Pa."

They walked back the way they'd come and found Darius waiting for them. "Come along with me to the mercantile, boys. Pa's already there trying to get a deal." He rolled his eyes and his brothers laughed. It was known that Parmenus Woodworth couldn't pass up a deal or the prospect of a good negotiation.

The boys opened the door and a bell tinkled, announcing their arrival. There was Pa, deep in debate over the price of coffee. He was working up a head of steam, gesticulating wildly, and the shopkeeper with a wispy mustache and weak chin nodded his head in agreement, but in the end, Parmenus couldn't sway the man to lower his prices. After a few moments, the man acknowledged their presence with a brief smile. "Be right with ya, gents."

"We're with him, Sir," Sandy said apologetically.

The man was visibly sweating as he tried to appease Pa. "Mister, I understand. The demand in these parts is great. I've got a family and I've got to make a decent living. I am not a greedy man, but it's a matter of you not fully understanding our local economy, Sir. I wish I could do better for you, but I cannot." Then he sliced the air with his hand and looked at Pa with a placid expression.

Sandy, Abijah, and Darius watched, fascinated by the interaction. It was obvious the man would not budge, and their father gave up trying to get a better deal. Pa shrugged, "I wouldn't be the man I am if I didn't try." He winked at his sons.

The kindly, albeit put-upon, shopkeeper assured Parmenus prices would be more affordable further from Sacramento. They settled on an abbreviated list of supplies that would have to make do until they arrived in Petaluma.

The Leffingwell party was now restocked and ready to finish their odyssey. A few families were headed to the gold diggings along the American River, but the remaining group would continue West. Tonight was to be their last campfire together, their last group meal and then it was time for goodbyes. The following morning at dawn they'd part ways.

Although most of the pioneers had wondered if following Sandy Woodworth was a foolhardy mistake, they were now effusive in their thanks and all wanted to shake hands with the man who'd led them safely and for the most part without incident to California.

James Cooper was last in line to shake Sandy's hand. "Proud to call you my friend. You took good care of us and I'll forever be in your debt."

"Stay in touch, James—write to me in Petaluma. I want to hear how the mining fares for you."

Twelve wagons now comprised the Leffingwell party. They'd stay together for remaining eighty-five miles to the little village of Petaluma. The pioneers were optimistic with food in their bellies and a replenished water supply. October arrived—harvest time, and shorter days. As the group got closer to the coast, they could smell and taste the salt air and feel it on their skin. They drove their wagons through hills and fields, marshes, and meadows.

The men hunted duck and quail, tried their luck with elk, and fished for trout and salmon. As they passed through grazing lands, they befriended the farmers and drank fresh milk after months of going without and gleaned windfall apples.

In the mornings, the heavy dew clung to everything and made bedrolls soggy; at night, dampness from the Pacific Ocean crept into their bones. They passed curious cone-shaped huts made from long strips of bark and saw the people they came to know as the Miwok tribe who inhabited them, and grand Adobes, and Ranchos belonging to Spanish and Mexican settlers.

The region was all the weary travelers could hope for. Petaluma was nestled in the golden hills, with majestic Mount Tamalpais to the south, and the Pacific Ocean to the west. The town bustled with activity, and Abijah felt comfortable the moment they arrived—something about the place and the fresh air was just right. There were shops and stables, wide streets, and wooden boardwalks. The mood differed from Sacramento—it was busy with commerce, but things seemed kinder. Folks were curious about the Leffingwell party, but greeted with a nod or a tip of the hat and moved along.

The Woodworth men asked around town and found out where they could camp until they found property to settle and where there was work to be had. As soon as they got comfortable, the matter of employment became their priority.

Sandy had letters of introduction from his Army Captain and Mr. Leffingwell, and secured a job driving stagecoach for Wells Fargo. Darius found work just as quickly at the livery stable. Abijah was left to tend to the livestock and help Ma in whatever way he could. Pa offered his services as an engineer and master builder, and was hired to work on projects in town.

It wasn't long before Parmenus' expertise was secured as a builder of a public house on Roblar Road. That job led to him hearing from one of the carpenters about a good piece of land in an area called Stony Point. It was close to town and had all the elements that he'd hoped for in the place he wanted to settle.

Chapter Eight
Stony Point

Marilla wasn't quite sure what she'd imagined would happen after her family arrived in California; she'd only focused on everyone surviving the journey. Everything about their lives now seemed different than it had back in Missouri—from the weather to the local economy. There were days she still felt like a stranger who'd never be accepted into the fold even as she was filled with the excitement for new possibilities and challenges. California was her home now and would be until the day she died, it was just a matter of accepting it into her heart.

She wasn't alone, not truly. Many of the area's inhabitants were pioneers, just like her family. When she got to feeling lonely or unsure of herself, Marilla remembered that her new neighbors were also grateful they'd arrived in this perfect place to make their dreams come true; that, like them, she was contributing to this new society. Like the others, her family was becoming part of a thriving landscape. The farmlands of the newly established Sonoma County were rich and would provide much needed produce to San Francisco via the Petaluma River. Sandy and Parmenus had done their research in finding a good place for their family to start over. Marilla was so proud when she thought about everything her family would accomplish.

The Woodworth's camped just at the edge of the river outside the village along with the other families from their sojourn West. Each evening they'd gather to share information. They discussed what was accomplished, who'd found work, and who needed help. Sandy was still matching up people with whatever assistance was required.

Wives and older children were now included in the bonfire discussions and Marilla sat next to Parmenus. "He's a natural leader, isn't he? I'm so proud of him," she whispered.

Her husband nodded. "He never asked for such responsibility, but neither does he shirk the obligation. Our journey showed him what he was made of."

There was a lull in the campfire conversation and then, Mr. Leffingwell asked if Abijah had time to see him about a team of oxen. Of course, their son agreed to help out.

"And Sandy's not the only one who's found what he's capable of. Abijah and Darius, too. Our sons are exceptional young men," Parmenus bragged quietly to his wife.

"Is California what you'd hoped for?"

He looked at his wife, as he answered, "It is more wonderful than I'd imagined. And you? Do you think you'll be happy here?"

She leaned against him, her head on his shoulder. "It's perfect here. I look forward to feeling part of the larger community. I know it will happen. In this place, I believe nearly anything is possible."

"Come with me tomorrow, I want you to see where we're going to make our home."

In the spring of 1854, Parmenus acquired 160 acres of land at Stony Point to homestead, approximately seven miles north of Petaluma. The family was close enough to town for convenience, but far enough so that when his sons could afford it, they would expand theirholdings.

"It's fair land, isn't it?" He asked and held Marilla's hand as they slowly traveled the acreage. It had rained the night before, but not enough to bog down the wheels. This morning the fog was low and thick but as noon approached, the features of the beautiful rolling hills were revealed.

Running through the back edge of the land was a fresh-water spring that branched into three streams, the largest of which ran southwest to the San Francisco Bay. The ground was hilly with good, rich soil.

Parmenus helped Marilla down from the wagon, and they climbed up the highest rise and turned in slow circles. The land would be perfect for fruit trees and he could imagine his orchards. There were varieties of oak, maple, and pine trees perfect for him to build his grand home.

He leaned over and felt the ground. "We'll be picking stones to clear this land." It would take the considerable effort of the whole family, but worth their labors.

"That we will. But we're in this together, Parmenus. We'll get the work done."

He pointed out the best spots to build and plant. Marilla loved hearing how filled with hope her husband had become. "We'll have enough lumber on this land to build what we need. God provides for us."

"I think you mean a lot of hard work will provide," she replied with eyebrow raised.

"Yes, as you say. But God always has his hand in things, Wife."

It was not long before Parmenus had a full work schedule. Word of his honesty and quality of craftsmanship spread in the area, and his skills and services were in high demand. He was hired to build bridges and public houses. The steady work meant money to pay his bills, and some to put away for the future. That left less time for his orchard and the home he would eventually build, but he already had his apple seedlings planted in carefully protected rows behind a storage shed he and Abijah had erected. Once they'd grown, he could move them to the orchard site.

"Marilla, it won't be long before the house is finished and we don't have to camp out. We'll be warm and dry by next winter."

"I'll be happy when we're indoors, Parmenus. We've looked forward to this time for so long and we're so close to achieving our dreams." Marilla looked at the big house taking shape. It was truly wonderful to behold—windows on all four sides, covered porches in the front and the back of the house. It was a two-story home with plenty of room for visiting family and several extra rooms that could be rented out to weary travelers when the public house down the road had reached capacity.

Abijah and his pa walked the acreage. Up one row and down the next, they checked each apple tree for disease. "How long before we have apples?" asked Abijah.

"This is why we started our seeds that first spring, Son. It takes some time but God willing, about eight years. I have a good feeling about it, though. The land is just right—the soil is rich. Pray the weather is with us."

Pa chose Gravenstein apples purposely. They were good right off the tree, baked in a pie, stewed into sauce or apple butter, and boiled into cider so as not to ferment. Abijah wished Pa would let a portion of the crop ferment into hard cider, but he wouldn't hear of it.

"Have you given any thought to where you want the root cellar?" The older man shrugged and pointed vaguely away from the edge of the orchard nearest the house.

"As soon as the spirit moves me, we'll dig."

"If you want it this year, we need to start soon before the weather goes poorly, Pa." Abijah felt a deep respect and love for his father, but waiting for God to decide where the root cellar belonged and when it should be dug was almost more than the young man could endure.

"We wait until He says it's right." Pa looked skyward, and Abijah made no further comment.

"I've been thinking lately, and maybe someday you'd like to take over our apple business when I'm too old. What do you say, Son?"

Abijah had known this conversation was coming and wished he could put it off, but he had to be honest about his feelings. He'd have to trust Pa would understand him. "You honor me, but I think maybe Samuel would like to stay here on the land when he's grown. Maybe you'll let him take over for you when it's time. You won't be ready for that anytime soon, will you, Pa?" Parmenus shook his head, but remained silent. "I've got something different planned for my life. So I hope, eventually, you'll let me go my own way."

If his father was disappointed with him, Abijah couldn't say. The older man looked at him appraisingly and laid a reassuring arm across his son's back. "Then, I guess it'll be up to our Samuel. Tell me about your plans."

"I'm working everything out in my head, Pa. I've got my heart set on being a dairy farmer. Now I just need to make sure I can make it happen."

"You're a hard worker—loyal and smart. Whatever you decide, I know you'll do well for yourself."

Abijah met up with his older brothers at the back edge of the Stony Point property. He had business to discuss with them and wanted the privacy found in the rows of apple trees. The day had started out damp and foggy, but the sun finally broke through, shaping into a beautiful fall day. He stopped in his tracks and looked up at his brothers. "We've got to get Pa's affairs settled with the property," he said.

"I take it you're speaking of the old land grants?" said Darius.

Abijah removed his battered hat and ran his hand over his wild head of hair. He'd have to get Ma to trim it soon. "I am and we need to make sure our parents aren't going to lose what they've worked so hard for."

Darius nodded in agreement. "What *we've* worked so hard for. Brother, I hear you, and I agree. I tried speaking with Pa about this, but he told me he had things well in hand."

"But, he doesn't," Abijah looked up at his brother, a serious expression on his otherwise cheerful face. "You know he means he's praying and waiting to hear from God. He settled the acreage but has no clear title and many folks hereabouts are in the same position. I'm worried we're going to be run off our own land."

Darius, whose property was also affected, explained what he'd learned for everyone's benefit. "From what I can gather, when California was acquired by the United States from Mexico, under the Treaty of Guadalupe de Hidalgo in 1848, the lands held by the Mexicans collapsed into chaos." He sat down on a rotten stump and pulled out a newspaper clipping he'd been carrying around. He handed it over to Sandy to read and then continued laying it all out. "Years later, newcomers, including our family, squatted on acreage previously held by Mexico. If we pursue this carefully, we'll eventually gain title and ownership of the land."

Abijah paced back and forth, trying to think everything through. He'd already read the article Sandy was perusing.

Darius went back to his explanation of the smaller grants in Northern California. The *Rancho Roblar de la Miseria*, or Ranch of the Oaks of Misery. This was the very land that the Woodworth's were improving. It belonged originally to General Mariano G. Vallejo who in turn, deeded it to one of his generals, Juan Padilla. Padilla was later run out of California for allegedly killing two Americans. Legal ownership was difficult to determine as General Vallejo and Padilla had sold portions of the land.

"To sum it up, this hinders clear title to the land. Our land, Brothers. And getting legal ownership of Stony Point will be challenging and costly for Pa."

Sandy had been silent during Darius' explanation, but when he finally spoke up, he got right to the heart of their problem. "Do we have the money to make the property legal?"

"We'll get it," said Abijah.

Darius nodded. "Whatever we need to do," he agreed. "Our parents shouldn't have a mortgage at their age."

It took some doing, but the Brothers Woodworth purchased the title to the Stony Point land in their father's name. Abijah worried about Pa's response and was glad the three of them could break the news together.

They told him as they helped him put the finishing touches on the root cellar.

"Why are you boys so serious? We've done a fair job on this cellar and your Ma's making a meal fit for kings." Parmenus looked at his boys. He knew something was weighing on them.

"We want to talk to you about the title for this property." Sandy explained the legal issues and why they felt it was vital to act quickly.

"Didn't want make you feel like we were going behind your back, Pa. We hope you see this as a good thing." Sandy smiled hopefully.

Pa looked at this sons. "It surprises me, but only because I didn't realize I needed to act so fast. I thought I had plenty of time. Thank you, boys, for always doing right by your Ma and me."

The relief Darius felt at his father's response was palpable. "We wanted to help. After all you and Ma have done for us over the years, it seemed right that we should do this for you."

"It is good land, and my heart would break to lose it. It will take some time to pay you back, but I will."

He said a quiet prayer of thanks before he and his eldest sons walked back to the house to see when dinner would be ready.

Parmenus decided to start his cider business before the first crop of apples came in. A neighbor had a Gravenstein orchard and had fallen upon hard times, so Parmenus bought the crop and began the process of producing cider. "Marilla, it's good practice for me. I can experiment on these and get everything refined by the time our first apples are ready."

"A very good idea, Husband, and you're helping our neighbor."

Some may have found his piety a bit hard to swallow, but as they came to know him, they saw that he was an honest man and that his heart was in the right place. Parmenus' council was sought on everything from barn-raising to crop rotation. He was a neighbor who could be counted on in good times, as well as during hardships.

Which was why he couldn't understand why the town fathers seemed so angry about his cider business. Marilla understood the problem but was hesitant to interfere with her husband's dealings on the matter. But finally, she could see that if there were ever to be any peace in her house, she needed to intervene.

Her husband was seated in front of the fireplace, reading the newspaper. "Parmenus, you must explain yourself to these people. They don't understand your intentions with the cider. They believe you are planning to sell spirits and that is why they are upset."

He looked over the top of his newspaper with eyebrows furled. "Now where would they have gotten this notion? Do they not know me to be a man of God? How can they think such things?"

God aside, her husband was stubborn as a mule but had to face the facts. People needed assurance he had no intentions of selling liquor. She sighed, hoping for the perfect words to soothe his frustration. "Husband, I think the good people of our community have misunderstood you. You must make them see. Our livelihood and standing depend on it."

Parmenus went to the meeting prepared to defend himself and make people see reason. Before he even began, he heard the grumbling.

"You can't sell your spirits here at the Washoe House, Woodworth," said one of the men. "It's not good for business." The building had just been completed; Parmenus had put his heart and soul in the construction. It would be open for business the summer of 1859 and the meeting was being held to plan the grand opening.

He tried to keep control of his emotions. He tried not to let their words hurt his feelings, but they did. Finally, he could stand it no longer. "Clearly, you gentlemen misunderstand my intentions. I have no plans of selling hard cider. I'm a man of God." He was met with silence. "I will boil my cider, and it will be crisp and delicious, and very refreshing. Perfect to offer travelers who stop at the guesthouse needing to quench their powerful thirst."

It was an honest mistake made by people who didn't know better, and while they all apologized and he accepted in good faith, their accusations still stung. Parmenus was in an ill temper upon his return home. He was not in the habit of having to explain himself to anyone but the Almighty.

That night, when the family had finished their supper, unknowing of his father's earlier troubles, Abijah mentioned that it might be a good idea if a portion of the crop *could* be fermented, as there was more money in the hard cider and perhaps it could be considered for medicinal purposes.

Of course, the lad would be made to see the error of his ways, and Parmenus felt a righteous anger rise as shouted at his son. "I'll have no part of this devil's business, nor will any of my household." He slammed his fist on the dining table, and got up so quickly that his chair tipped over. For his part, the boy blushed in embarrassment, dropped the subject after apologizing profusely and hastily excused himself.

Parmenus caught up later that evening with Abijah who was cleaning stalls in the barn.

"I'm sorry for what I said, Pa. I don't know what I was thinking, except that I was trying to come up with ideas to make money. I meant no disrespect." Abijah stopped his shoveling and looked his father in the eye.

It was clear that the boy was sincere and Parmenus knew at that moment that no further action on his part was necessary. "I forgive you, Abijah, but you must understand I would never do such a thing."

Once the men in his community realized he had no intentions of selling liquor, they agreed to let him set up shop and there were no hard feelings about the misunderstanding. The roadhouse was located at the intersections of Roblar Road and Stony Point, and served as an essential stagecoach stop that connected the towns of Petaluma, Santa Rosa, and Bodega. Woodworth's Boiled Cider was a treat enjoyed by travelers and locals alike.

Chapter Nine
Christmas at Stony Point

Between the successful cider business and the engineering jobs Parmenus had completed, the construction of the home at Stony Point wrapped up right before Christmas. The elder Woodworth's were delighted to celebrate their bounty with the family. The four eldest children and their spouses came to spend the holiday.

Marilla and her daughters made roast duck and goose. They had beans and sweet potatoes and mashed potatoes with gravy, corn muffins with butter, applesauce, and apple pies.

The weather that Christmas Eve was cold and windy and the fog had come in from the ocean, making it impossible to see farther than a few feet ahead on the road. No one would be driving their buggy home tonight.

After dinner, everyone gathered in the parlor for stories. It had been a very long time since Parmenus played the storyteller, and the family enjoyed resuming their holiday tradition. The wood in the fireplace crackled and the flames cast warm light and everyone was safe and well fed and grateful.

"It's been a few years since I've told this tale, and since the last time, we are many more in number. This is the history of our family, our ancestors, and how we came to be. Listen closely and mark my words," Parmenus began. It was a solemn tale and the room was silent as he began a story that had been handed down over the generations.

"Back so long ago that hardly anyone can remember, there was a group of Englishmen called the Men Of Kent. It was told that they had the reputations of honorable and resolute men. In 1633, they bravely sailed the ocean on a tall-ship to begin a great adventure in

America. After harsh weather and months at sea, they arrived feeling weakened yet filled with optimism at Plymouth, Massachusetts. One was called Walter Woodworth, and he was my great-great-great-grandfather. Walter was unable to pay for the voyage from England, so came to America as an indentured servant. He traveled from Plymouth to Scituate, Massachusetts, and there he lived and raised his family. He worked to better himself and to pay his servitude. And though it took seven years, he was declared a free man in 1640 and his worldly possessions included his purse, apparel, and books. He worked as a surveyor of highways, as an arbiter, and served on the coroner's jury. After completing this duties, he was once again listed as a free man with the right to bear arms in Plymouth in 1642. Twenty years later, he was granted 60 acres of land in Scituate. In the year 1686, at the good age of 74, he went to his great reward.

"Walter had a son named Ben, born in 1649. Ben was my great-great-grandfather, and he lived to be 79. He had a son, Ezekiel, my great-grandfather who lived only 49 short years. Ezekiel left Massachusetts with his family and moved to Connecticut. His son, Peleg, my grandfather, was born in 1732. He was a soldier in the French and Indian War. Peleg lived until the age of 79. His son, my father, was named James. James was born in 1766 and lived in Connecticut until he moved to Painesville, Ohio. During the Revolution, he was an Ensign of the 4th Company in the 12th Regiment of Connecticut. When his service was up, he lived for a time in upstate New York. He was one of sixteen children and worked hard as a farmer. To this day, my father still lives in Ohio, and he is a very old man nearing the age of 89.

"I was born in 1806 in New York, and my father named me Parmenus Newton Woodworth. When I was but a child, my father sold me into servitude and in that way, I learned my trade. I became a builder of bridges, of barns, of homes large and small. I learned to do whatever God required to earn my keep. I married a woman I loved, named Marilla, and she gave me seven children. Four boys and three girls, and each child, was intelligent and strong. In 1853, the Lord spoke to me and told me it was time to bring my family across America to California to find prosperity, and work the land here at Stony Point.

"Someday, you will tell your children and grandchildren about our family, so I hope you've listened well to the story of the Men Of Kent, the Woodworth men."

No sooner had Parmenus finished than his children wanted another story. "Now tell us about the talking animals," Martha said with a smile.

"Yes, please tell it," said Marilla.

Parmenus stood illuminated by the firelight and Marilla listened, just as enrapt as his children. "You must have noticed," he began, "the wreaths your mother and I made to hang on the barn. We cut fir boughs and the branches from the gum trees and sprigs of holly and twisted them together. Then we tied them with red ribbons and hung them on the barn doors. We put them up because the barns are symbolic of the holy night, when Jesus was born in a mere humble manger.

"On that most holy night when Christmas Eve became Christmas Morning, all the animals attending the birth of the baby Jesus were given the magical gift of speech. The doves up high in the rafters could speak, their words as soft as the fluttering of their wings. The lambs, oxen, cows, goats, and even the donkeys could speak and they were so honored by their gift that real tears came to their eyes. The rabbits, the chickens, and the little barn mice watching from their place in the corner—they spoke with small, quick voices. And lastly, the camels, who had carried their wise men such a long way; they could speak with voices deep and kind.

"It is our wish, and our truest desire that when we hang our wreaths and the midnight hour is upon us, our animals might speak, too, if we have faith, if we believe."

Parmenus finished with a smile and his wife kissed his cheek. "That was beautiful, Husband."

The youngest of the children yawned and rubbed at their eyes; it was time for bed. It was good to have everyone at home and the family had many blessings. Tomorrow they would celebrate Christ's birthday. It would be beautiful and solemn. But tonight was for family, for renewing the ties that bound them together so firmly.

Abijah & Abigail (Abby) Hall
Woodworth
(1837 – 1930) (1842 – 1924)
|
Fred
(1869 – 1908)
Ralph
(1871 – Living)

Chapter Ten
Tomales Dreams

Long before the Woodworth family came to California, Abijah had a prophetic dream in which he saw strange visions of his future. He recognized himself as a landowner in a beautiful but unknown place of high green hills and clear streams. He watched from above as a forest of trees grew before his eyes. He saw the grand ranch he'd built with his own hands and heard milk cows lowing in the distance. His children were healthy, running, and playing in the velvety grass. He got a glimpse of his sons as older boys, smiling and proud. There was a woman, a serious, dark haired woman of small stature working as hard as the man by his side—he knew they belonged together.

Part of the dream came from the story his father told of the Woodworth lineage. It gave him such a sense of connectedness, not only to his people, but to the land. He imagined Walter Woodworth as he sailed across the ocean to America and promised himself that his dream would include a sailor, a sword, and an anchor to mark their lives. But he did not know yet how that might happen.

The first time he had this dream, Abijah knew that his future had been laid out before him by some power greater than himself. It didn't matter that his siblings couldn't understand his experience, he knew what it meant. Over the next few years, Abijah's dream came to him repeatedly, and each time, he awoke with renewed resolve and knew he would do anything to make this his reality.

Abijah and his pa sat up late talking by the fire one evening. He sensed the older man was in good spirits and decided now was as good a time as any for him to start talking about his future.

"Pa, there's good land near T...T- Tomales Bay, and I know it's the perfect place for me. I met Mr. Marshall, the owner. He's a good man and I think he'll sell the land at a f...f-fair price." His father was silent and Abijah felt his heartbeat keeping time with the clock on the mantel. He began to wonder if he'd picked the wrong time to speak of his future.

"Your Ma and I had our hearts set on you settling near us here at Stony Point. We wanted you to farm the land, plant more apple orchards." Abijah felt his mouth go dry. "I know you don't want to be a farmer, but I prayed maybe you'd change your mind."

He disliked disappointing his parents, but he was determined to make his own way. "You've built Stony Point into a fine home. You and Ma are important members of the community. I want the same opportunity. The cider business has served our family well, but I have something different in mind. I want to be a dairyman and I want to build my future with my own hands. I'm gonna raise milk cows and sheep and chickens, and maybe pigs too. And I won't be too far from Stony Point, Pa. We can visit whenever we like."

Father and son sat quietly for a long time, pondering. Finally, Abijah could wait no longer, "What do you say, Pa, will you buy back my acreage at Stony Point? It will give me a good start, and I have a plan to make the rest of the money I need."

"As much as I hate to see you go, you are right, Abijah. You've got to make your own way in this life, just as I did mine. I left my Pa back in Ohio. Do you remember him?" Abijah nodded. "Well, he was a hard man, but he never did begrudge me the chance to make my mark. I have tried to set the right example for you boys. I tried to be an honest, God-fearing man, and I'm proud to have raised strong, good men."

"Yes, sir," Abijah agreed.

"Tell me how you'll go about getting this dairy business working."

"I've saved a little money but not enough. If you buy back my land, it will put me in position to give Mr. Marshall some earnest money. After that, each time I complete a job, I'll put money in the bank."

"What will you do for work?"

"I found work in Virginia City at the Comstock Silver Mine. Once I've saved enough money, I'll quit the mine and buy me a team of oxen and a sturdy wagon. I'm going to make the rest of my money hauling supplies from San Francisco up to the miners. Placerville,

Angels Camp, Sonora—wherever I can find work, that's where I'll haul."

"Mining is dangerous work, Son. It's a hard life, and there will be temptations in that town, unlike any you've ever known. Your mother will have plenty to say about it; better be prepared."

His pa looked worried. Abijah thought his talk of mining might have soured the support he was counting on. He plowed ahead, unable to keep the enthusiasm out of his voice. "Pa, I know, and I'll be alright. The plan is to make my money and get out. Every penny I save is a penny toward my dreams. I don't relish working in the mines, but it's the best way for me to get started."

Abijah noticed a slight shift in his father's demeanor and knew he'd won him over. He had his blessing.

There were a thousand things that could kill a man down there—cave-ins, underground flooding and fires. Deep in the shafts, when the rock was penetrated, the resultant steam reached temperatures that would boil as the water filled the tunnels. Boiling to death was a horrendous fate but Abijah's most current fear was going blind down in the pit. It was always on his mind that if he worked in Virginia City too long, this might be his fate. It became something of an obsession for him that would only be cured when he no longer worked down in the hole. When end of day came, and he was hoisted back up, he looked up to the gathering stars and counted his blessings–still alive and one day closer to his dream.

If, by luck or grace, a man managed to survive laboring in the dark, life above ground held treachery of a different sort. Abijah had learned to quicken his pace as he made his way through town. Stray bullets had a way of finding those who moved with ill intent or without purpose; he had seen it with his own eyes during his first week. *I'll certainly not tell Ma and Pa about what goes on in this place,* he decided right then and there.

All a man had to do was pay attention and he'd be witness to all manner of brawls that spilled from the saloons out onto the streets. At first, watching *the show,* as it was called, at night after work was entertainment of a sort, but Abijah quickly saw that it was easy to be in the wrong place at the wrong time. A ne'er-do-well given to evil deeds would surely rob you or worse, if he thought you had some money.

After supper one night, Abijah turned left instead of right and found himself just outside the saloon. He wasn't a hard drinking man, but he was weary and hoped to find some entertainment.

Upon entering the establishment, he'd hesitated a little too long before the swinging doors, and someone behind him jammed their elbow into his back and pushed hard enough to knock him into the room. That got everyone's attention for about two seconds; Abijah chuckled to himself, and made his way up to the bar. He asked for a beer, was given one, and then turned to face the room. In walked a fellow boarder from his rooming house Michael Flaherty. Abijah waved him over. "Can I buy you a drink?"

"I'll never say no to a free drink, Abijah." Michael ordered a whiskey and nodded his thanks. "What brings you here, friend?"

Abijah looked around and shrugged. "I miss my kin. Not that they'd ever come to a place like this, mind you, but sometimes I don't want to be by m'self. And I do enjoy a drink on occasion."

Michael finished his drink and ordered the bottle.

Abijah laughed and caught the bartender's attention. "He's on his own after the first drink, Sir. I'll settle up if you don't mind." He laid down his money and the bartender nodded his understanding. "Sorry to be so thrifty, Michael, but I don't plan to be in this place longer than I have to."

"Oh, that's just fine. I thank you for the drink. Speaking of places you don't plan to be for long, did you mean in this establishment or Virginia City?"

"Yes," Abijah joked. "But seriously, friend, the sooner I can make my money and get home, the happier I'll be."

"Smart. I've seen many men parted with their money or their lives around here."

Abijah reflected, "I'm here to save not to spend, but some days that's just not possible. My ma would cry herself to sleep if she could see me now." He shook his head. "Sorry, didn't mean to bring our conversation down. I'd better git. I'll see you tomorrow, Michael." He shook the man's hand and left the saloon.

On his way back to the rooming house, Abijah was deep in thought and not paying attention to who passed him on the boardwalk. After a moment, he sensed another's presence, looked up and saw that he was walking in the direct path of another man. He stepped quickly to one side and the man swayed in the opposite direction. As he did so, Abijah laid a finger to the brim of his hat, and gave the man a little nod. "Good evening to you, Sir."

The man, who reeked of tobacco and alcohol, took exception to the friendly greeting. "Who the hell are you?" He turned back and came round again. Abijah felt an iron fist as it connected with his right cheekbone.

The unprovoked violence came as a shock to Abijah but he braced himself for more of the same. He shouted, "Get out of my way, Fellah. Leave me alone."

His teetering opponent might have been drunk but it was clear, he was just getting started. Although he was small of stature, Abijah was well capable of looking after himself with his fists, having two much larger older brothers. He landed a solid blow and watched as the drunken man sank to ground. Down, but miraculously not out, the drunk shouted loudly, "I'll get ya, ye bastard!" But Abijah had other plans and managed to extricate himself before more bodily harm was done to either him or the drunk.

Abijah, looked around, hoping to have avoided the interest of the sheriff, and saw that no one cared about his petty squabbles. He was confident he'd have a shiner the next day, and he was already feeling the pain, but the altercation didn't frighten him. Rather he took it as a lesson.

The next morning at Sunday breakfast, Mrs. Baker sat in her place at the head of the table in judgment. After they'd finished grace, she looked at Abijah with a raised eyebrow. "You've been fighting, Sir, and I'll not have that in my house. The rules were explained."

"I'm sorry, Ma'am. I was accosted last night after dinner. I tried to get away before it came to blows, but the other man had different plans."

"You're forgiven this time. But next time, you're out. Understand?" She narrowed her eyes at him.

"Thank you for giving me another chance." Of anyone he'd encountered, Abijah thought Mrs. Baker was the one to watch out for.

Abijah purchased postcards for both Sandy and Darius. He wrote similar notes on each.

Greetings, Brother!

Got into my first scrap in town. Your training is appreciated. I made out moderately well. A colorful bruise is all I have to show for my troubles —that and a dressing down by my landlady. You can tell Pa when you see him, but please don't tell Ma.

Yours - Abijah.

After that, he kept to himself and watched out for drunkards. He stayed out of the gambling houses, didn't drink to excess, and gave the women in town a wide berth.

Working down in the pit, no one talked much. Everyone concentrated instead on doing their jobs and surviving the dangers.

As he'd written to his Pa, *I know who I can be friends with and who to avoid down in the pit. That's the best I can do.*

After-hours was another matter and Abijah found a couple miners he enjoyed visiting with—Stuart Granger and Allen Thompson. They got together Sundays after lunch to play chess on old crates they set up next to the churchyard. There was always an odd man out, but the conversation was so lively that it didn't seem to matter. All three of them had yarns to spin and jokes to tell.

"Tell us about finding your land back home, Abijah," Stuart asked him. "I want to hear about your dairy farm dreams."

At first, Abijah thought the men were poking fun at him, but then he realized that his experiences were different than theirs had been and they were just as curious as they were friendly. So he told them about his family, their journey West, his hopes and dreams, and they told him theirs. "I did worry about my pa when I told him my plans. I don't want to abandon him, but I need to live my own life, you understand, right?"

Allen nodded agreement. "Of course, I do. My ma died when I was a boy and I ran away from home when I was thirteen. Pa was a drunkard, mean, and he beat me and my ma. After she passed, I couldn't get away from him fast enough. I made my way out West. Working the whole way, but I made it and here I am to tell the tale."

Abijah couldn't fathom having a father who would beat his ma. It made him feel grateful and sorrowful at the same time. "You ever think about getting m...married, Allen?"

"Don't know as that's in the cards for me. Maybe someday?" Abijah's friend looked at him, the sadness he felt coming through.

"I'll get married, I suppose," Stuart chimed in. "But I haven't met the right woman yet."

When he wrote home, he told of those miners and their lives. He was glad to have something diverting that explained a bit about Virginia City without having to trouble the folks with the often dangerous life he was leading. He never told them of his close calls on the streets or in the mines, there was no point in worrying his mother needlessly.

"Had a little cave-in yesterday, did you?" asked Allen.

"Lord, yes we d...did." Abijah had had the hardest time falling asleep the night before. The cave-in had frightened him; made him feel every bit of his mortality. "Boys, I'll tell you, I discovered what it was to be afraid for my life. And before you ask me, no, I am not going to tell my ma and pa about this." Abijah shivered with the memory.

"Eventually it happens to all of us. Pray we finish our time down there before the big cave-in." Stuart shook his head.

Abijah labored in the dark and damp for two years and once he'd saved the amount of money he needed, he said his good-byes, packed up his belongings, and hastily made his way home.

Now, it was time for him to put the next part of his plan in motion and begin his hauling business. Word got around and he had the well-deserved reputation of an honest and forthright man. He could have worked hauling bars of gold or coin, but he refused. His older brother, Sandy, was shot in the face while driving a stagecoach for Wells Fargo just north of Santa Rosa, and Abijah refused to put his life in that kind of danger.

Ike Hall was a wealthy wool broker in San Francisco, and he was looking for a trustworthy man to haul blankets to gold country. Abijah was recommended as a skilled teamster and Ike liked the young man immediately.

"Mr. Hall, I'll get those blankets to their destination safe and s...s-sound. I worked at the Comstock Mine, and I know the road to Virginia City like the back of my hand. And I'll do it for a fair price —not the cheapest, mind you, but I believe you get what you pay for. I'm honest, and I keep my promises. Do we have a d...d-deal?" The two men shook hands, and an agreement was struck.

Abby Hall had been talked into attending a dance in Bloomfield. This was not her idea of suitable diversion, but her only friend in California had requested she go along and so she did. She'd made all of the excuses including her unwillingness to make the seven-mile trip from Fallon, where she lived and taught school, but Margaret pushed and now they were pulling up to the community hall for a night of entertainment. Abby would not be dancing and so she decided her role for the night would be to serve as Margaret's chaperone.

The two entered the dance and saw that attendance was excellent. The evening was open to one and all—young people hoping to meet someone special, older married couples, and children who ran about the dance floor excitedly. Abby expected to see at least one of her brothers this night, and Margaret's parents had already arrived.

They waved to Abby and Margaret and the girls waved back. It was loud and chaotic and not at all how Abby had hoped to spend her Saturday night.

"And Abby, I can be your chaperone if you like." Margaret clapped her hands gleefully and giggled at their prospects.

Margaret did a little spin to show off her beautiful, cornflower blue silk dress. Abby was dressed plainly in her best light grey silk adorned with a small lace collar and felt she looked very presentable. She knew that compared to her friend, she was like a little field mouse but it didn't bother her overly much.

"You know me, Margaret. I will not do anything that would cause me to need a chaperone." Honestly, the girl was just as silly as she could be. But there were few choices in female companionship in the little hamlet of Fallon, and there *was* something winning about Margaret's personality. And sometimes, she said the most outrageous things.

"You simply must give yourself up to the night, Abby, and please do not be so serious." Now, Margaret scanned the dance-goers and stopped when she saw the young man she had her sights set upon. She grabbed at Abby's elbow and let out a dramatic sigh. "Oh, look at him. He's the most handsome—Jacob Patton—I should be like to be Mrs. Jacob Patton."

Abby nodded when she saw the object of her friend's affection but did not see what was so special about him. She returned to their previous conversation. "But Margaret, I *am* a serious woman." But her friend was making a fuss at her desired beau. Abby watched in secret fascination as the eyelashes were expertly fluttered and another round of tinkling giggles were issued.

Margaret continued trying to school Abby. "Men do not like a woman with a downturned mouth. Smile. Put some effort in, girl." She now demonstrated by laughing as though she'd heard the funniest thing toward Mr. Patton's direction.

Abby tried on a small smile just to appease her friend. "I *am* trying. But Margaret, I will not giggle. I have never giggled."

"And don't speak with all of your *'thees'* and *'thous'*. Don't you want to marry?"

Abby wondered how the way she spoke could have bearing on whether or not she found a suitable husband. She chuckled softly. With Margaret, everything circled back to marriage.

"Not particularly." Abby couldn't imagine being someone's wife although it was inevitable that eventually she'd go down that road just like every other woman.

Margaret narrowed her eyes and looked at her friend. "I think you are being purposely droll and you really must stop it. Ah, here he comes. He's going to ask me to dance, I just know it." And he did.

Margaret could be utterly exhausting and Abby watched her friend take the dance floor with a swish of her skirts, grateful to be left in peace. Now that she was alone, she allowed herself to glance around to see if anyone there caught her eye. *As if that were possible*, she thought, irritated with herself.

But there he was. A handsome young man. And he was familiar to her, but Abby wasn't sure how that was possible. She supposed she'd seen him in Petaluma or perhaps he was an associate of one of her brothers. Whatever the case, he was well dressed but not overly so, wearing polished boots that were well worn without being shabby. He was just a few inches taller than she was and looked a bit thin, but still possessed an obvious strength. Abby could tell he worked hard for a living. A farmer, perhaps? Not much of a surprise considering where they lived. Brown hair, ruddy complexion, eyes that flashed with humor.

Abby was still wondering about this mystery man when he walked out of the big hall. She was unaccountably disappointed. But then she noticed him again and he was moving in her direction, carrying two drinks.

"Hello there. I noticed you on your own and thought you might like a cup of punch. I'm Abijah W...Woodworth."

"Thank you. I'm Abby Hall." She took the proffered drink and sipped as daintily as she knew how.

"I'm very pleased to meet you. Say, are you kin to Ike Hall, the wool broker?"

"I am. He is my brother. How do you know Ike?"

"I haul blankets for him up to the gold fields."

"Oh." Abby was suddenly at a strange loss for words but knew she should say something. "That must be hard work." *What a stupid thing to say*, she thought.

"Well, it can be. But it's a good job and I like working for Mr. Hall. He's a very good business man." Abby thought she'd like to hear what her brother thought of Abijah Woodworth. She wondered if he would be coming tonight.

"There's my friend Margaret Pierce and Mr. Patton. May I introduce you?" Which was the last thing Abby wanted to do, but she supposed she should be polite. They were making their way towards her and Abijah. She said his name silently, and felt a thrill.

Margaret gave Abby a raised eyebrow, obviously surprised that her shy friend found someone. Abby caught the looked and shrugged nonchalantly as introductions were made between the four.

"We were going to get some fresh air outside, would you care to join us?" said Mr. Patton.

"I think not," Abby replied. Her voice must have sounded cold but the truth was, she wanted to visit with Abijah—not Abijah, Margaret, and Mr. Patton. Luckily, Margaret was so entranced by her new suitor that Abby didn't think the slight had even been noticed.

"I thought I'd ask Miss Hall for a dance." Abijah wasn't sure what had transpired between the two ladies, but he decided to intervene before any further discomfort ensued. The music was a waltz and after some initial clumsiness, they came together as though they'd been dancing together for years.

"Thank you. I really have had enough of Margaret's prattle for the evening. She is my friend, but she's impossible when she's with a new beau." Abby stopped abruptly, not quite sure why she spoken with such candor. She hoped Abijah didn't think she made it a habit of gossiping about so-called friends. He didn't reply, but she felt a moment of relief when she heard him chuckle.

Abijah and Abby spent the rest of the evening dancing and getting to know each other but, too soon, it was time for them to go their separate ways. It was evident that neither of them wished to part. Abijah asked if he could call on her again, and Abby agreed. She said a hasty goodnight because Margaret waited impatiently by the buggy Abby had borrowed from her brother.

"You had a nice evening," Margaret observed. And Abby could tell her friend would try to worm any information out that she could.

"Yes, I did. And you?"

"Well, *I* have a new beau. Do *you*?"

Abby thought a moment trying to decide whether to give in and tell or to keep it to herself. "I think I might," she conceded.

He watched unseen for a few moments as Abby restored order to her schoolhouse.

Abijah finally cleared his throat nervously. "Hello, Miss Abby," he greeted.

"Hello. What brings you here, Mr. Woodworth?" Abby seemed surprised by his appearance at the side door of the school. Abijah hoped he hadn't made an error in judgment.

She'd been straightening the rows of desks and cleaning the blackboard when her visitor made his presence known. Suddenly, she seemed to have forgotten what she was doing and stood silently looking at Abijah.

"I've come to find out if you'd like to visit my family home—they are anxious to meet you."

"That sounds nice, but are you sure it's a good idea? We've only just become acquainted." Abby wasn't sure she was ready to meet his family.

"I know it seems a bit soon, but you are all I talk about." Abijah felt his face flush with his declaration.

Please say yes, he thought. "Well, if that's the case, I would be delighted," Abby answered.

"Is this Saturday too soon? I'd bring you back home early Sunday evening. My family lives at Stony Point, so it's a bit of a distance, but we have plenty of room for guests. Ma thought you might like to share a room with my sister, Liza."

"My goodness. You've got everything planned out. Shall I bring a cake?" Abijah thought the blush rising in Abby's cheeks was lovely.

"Oh, most assuredly, we all enjoy dessert. I shall pick you up on Saturday morning at eleven."

"I will make a picnic lunch for our travels."

Abijah hoped she was a good cook. "If it's not too much trouble, that would be grand."

Abby went back to straightening the children's desks but she looked a bit distracted. *Did I do that?* he wondered. "If you are ready to go home now, I'd be honored to take you in my buggy if you'd like."

"I would appreciate that. I'll be ready in just a few minutes. I like to get my classroom just right so that all is ready when I arrive in the morning."

"Can I help you with anything, Miss Abby?"

"You can bring in some wood for the stove, if you please."

Abijah brought in an armload of wood, filled the potbellied stove, and put the rest in a metal bucket.

"There, all ready for tomorrow," he stated.

When he dropped her off at her home, Abijah felt like whooping and hollering he was so happy. Then he said aloud to no one and everyone, "I'm going to marry her!"

The visit with Abijah's family went well, Abby supposed. There *were* some key differences between her and the Woodworth's. She was not one to talk much, and Abijah's family all seemed to speak at once and continually. She hardly knew how anyone could follow their conversations. They were a jovial lot. Meals seemed to be chaotic but good-natured affairs at this house. Parmenus offered a rather long-winded prayer of thanks before the family began eating. Abby bowed her head and sat at quiet attention during grace in deference to the family belief. Her family observed momentary silence before meals, but rarely had her father or her brothers said anything in the prayerful way out loud. It was the way of Quakers to eat without the interruption of conversation.

When Abijah's father finished his prayer and said an 'Amen,' an immediate cacophony of excited voices broke in, and Abby was taken by surprise. She had never experienced anything like it in her life, and although she didn't dislike it, she didn't quite understand what was happening or if she should be inserting herself into conversation. She opted to observe silently.

As everyone had finished eating their dinner, Marilla broke into the din. "Children, quiet down. I have a question for our guest. Abigail, would you mind telling us about your trip from New York to California? It must have been a grand adventure."

Abby set her knife and fork down on her plate to indicate that she had finished eating. Marilla noticed and got Liza's attention and the young girl cleared away the dishes.

Suddenly, all eyes were upon her and she was expected to give a performance of sorts. Abby was not comfortable being the center of attention but she decided she'd do as requested. She looked toward Abijah for any indication of how she should proceed. He was of little help and stared at her unabashedly with his elbows on the table and his chin propped on his hands.

She tried to calm her nerves. "Well, it was a very long trip and made longer by the fact that we waited in Panama City far longer than we had anticipated. We began our travels by ship, then on a boat, a train, and finally back on a ship," Abby began.

"I've never been on a ship, only a barge across a river when we came out West," said Marilla and grabbed Abby's hands and gave them a squeeze. *Strange,* Abby thought, *these people were quite physical with one another. So unlike my family.*

"It was my first time too, Ma'am. We sailed out of New York on the Clipper Ship Diana, bound for Porto Bella, Panama. Mama and I were seasick the whole way. We stayed in a tiny room with four other women who were also dreadfully ill. There were only six females on the entire ship, so the captain thought we'd be more comfortable if we were to share the same room. I can tell you honestly that we were not.

"My brother, Ike, and my brother, Daniel, had a room to themselves, but they were also sick and didn't enjoy the trip either. Still, I was jealous that it was just the two of them and told them so. I should mention that my brother, Brad, was already in California." Abby stopped, to gather her thoughts. She supposed she really needn't give much more than just the most important details.

"Do continue," prompted Parmenus.

"It was wearisome, but I kept thinking about California, and it made the terrible times not quite so terrible. After we'd arrived in Porto Bella, we traveled in a small boat up the Charges River to where we boarded the Trans-Isthmian Railroad. The train was not intended to accommodate people. It was for carrying freight bound for the gold mines of California.

"Unfortunately, our compartment was infested with fleas, which made a meal out of us all. Thankfully, it was only a one-day journey to Panama City. But it wasn't long before we were covered in bites." Abby broke off again. She'd gotten off topic thinking about those accursed fleas. "My apologies for the uncouth description." She felt her cheeks heat and hoped Mrs. Woodworth wouldn't be put off by her talk of such bodily things. Abijah smiled at her in encouragement. "The train traveled up a rise of 275 feet, and then at the top, our engine was replaced, and we began the descent to the Pacific side."

"My goodness, did you keep a diary of your adventures?" asked Marilla.

"I did so that I wouldn't forget any details. Once we'd arrived in Panama City, we were informed that our ship had been delayed by five days. I hoped to spend some time seeing the city, but my brothers had gone out for a walk and reported back that all was chaos, and many diseases ran rampant. Mother decided it would be far too dangerous to venture out. I desperately wished to explore, but fear of contracting cholera or yellow fever tempered any disappointment—I suppose it was for the best. In the end, about the only thing I saw of Panama City was the inside of our hotel, which wasn't very nice."

"The whole trip sounds terrible," said Mary.

"Some parts of it were awful, but never fear," Abby gave a little chuckle, "it did get better. Once we were aboard the Falcon, we sailed north and west towards California and our travels improved remarkably. We were able to enjoy the sea air and the vastness of the Pacific Ocean. It was quite bracing and pleasant. None of us experienced the seasickness that we did on the Atlantic side coming from New York.

"Our rooms were not grand, but they were clean and quite comfortable and no fleas. We slept well at night and in the morning got up and took breakfast in the dining quarters. We walked the length of the ship back and forth, and the wind off the water felt clean and healthful. I spent many hours reading on deck and occasionally spoke with other passengers about their journeys.

"And then, finally, we approached San Francisco. The city was shrouded in fog, and we could not make out the details of the place. But the crew and captain assured me that it was a wonderful city to visit. When we finally arrived at Bodega Bay, we were grateful to stand on firm land once again."

"Now that you are here, how do you like C...C- California?" asked Abijah.

"I like it very much. I don't miss the snow and the cold of the East Coast or the humidity of New York in the summer. I do miss my sister and the meeting house where my people worship. But I am very pleased to be here. The journey was worth it." Abby smiled and blushed.

"That was quite a tale, Abigail," said Darius.

"Yes," said Parmenus. "Thank you so much for telling us about your adventures."

"My goodness, I don't think I've ever spoken so much at one time," Abby said with surprise.

Marilla gave the girl a friendly smile. "I'm so happy you told us your story. It was fascinating and so different from our Westward journey to California. Do you think you'll ever go back to visit New York?"

"Someday, I hope to. I recently read an article in a San Francisco newspaper about travel across the continent. It stated that it wouldn't be long before California was connected to the rest of the country by train. And then there will be no need for the dangerous crossings such as our families experienced."

Abijah wondered if Abby's family would approve of him since he hadn't much formal education. He decided it was time for him to declare himself, and he was nervous about their reaction. He needn't have had any fear about his acceptability, and him not being Quaker didn't seem to make any difference to the Hall brothers. They were more interested in how he conducted his business affairs than the state of his soul. They judged him to be a hardworking and tenacious man who was honest in ways of business. If Abby liked him, they saw no reason why there couldn't be a match.

Abijah's family found Abby to be a thoughtful, serious young woman. She didn't seem to be one accustomed to smiles or jokes in the way their son was, and they wondered what the two might have in common.

"I like your young lady. But heaven's above, what do you two talk about?" asked Marilla. She was rolling out dough for an apple pie and Abijah sat in the kitchen reading the newspaper. Parmenus was in town on business, so Marilla thought it was the perfect time to talk to her son about Abby Hall.

Abijah looked over his newspaper in surprise. "What do you mean, Ma? We talk about everything. C...c-cows, dairy farming, family, business matters, education, our future."

"I imagine Abigail must be a knowledgeable young lady, being that she is a teacher, and I'm sure she has had an outstanding education. But Abijah, for a female, some things are more important than education."

"What do you mean, Ma? You've spoken with her. She may not be like my sisters, but she's plenty interesting."

"I mean, can you laugh together when the journey becomes difficult? Can you comfort one another when life feels unbearable? Do you trust one another?"

"She does have a sense of humor, very subtle. I think it comes from being a teacher—she's got to be so serious with the children. But I'll warm her up. I know I can."

"I hope so, 'Bije. I want you to find a good match—someone who will be your friend and your partner." His mother paused a moment, trying to find the right words. "What about her religion? Will you become a Quaker? I worry, Pa might disapprove."

"She hasn't said much about religion, but you're right, it's high time we talked about it. There are no Quaker meeting houses here, but I would never ask her to take a different faith. You know I don't hold much stock in church-going. I know God's listening, but I don't believe he only listens to those in church."

It was a beautiful spring day, and the young couple enjoyed their ride in Abijah's buggy. The air was sweet with the scent of spring's wildflowers, and everywhere the grass was lush and soft. His horse picked her way carefully up a steep cattle trail to the top of the hill.

They'd brought along a picnic and Abijah was excited to show off his land.

"Whoa, Princess." They stopped to appreciate their surroundings, and Abijah produced two apples from his coat—one for his pa's old chestnut mare and one to share with Abby.

"Isn't it beautiful up here, Abby?" Abijah hopped out of the carriage and then reached up to help her down. They walked about fifty feet and found themselves looking down over the edge of a cliff to green hills below.

Princess made quick work of her apple and wandered to a patch of sweet clover. Abby smiled and tucked the second apple away in the picnic basket with the rest of their lunch.

"Yes, but it seems like we're very far from everything." Abijah steadied her as Abby stumbled and looked into her dark eyes.

"Are you alright?" Abijah took her hand in his.

"Yes, just a bit dizzy. I'll be fine. I'm bothered by heights."

"I admit, it does feel remote but look this way," he looked over her shoulder and pointed westward. "This way is the ocean, just over the next rise. To the northwest, about two miles, is T...T-Tomales—there's a mercantile and a few other businesses there. East of Tomales, is Bloomfield, where we met at the dance. Back that way is Petaluma, about sixteen miles. And San Francisco is 60 miles south."

"I'm not an expert, but it is beautiful here. And I know you know what you need in the way of land. I think you've chosen well."

Abijah gathered his courage before continuing. This was possibly the most important conversation he'd ever have. Abby looked patiently at him.

"I'm buying this land, Abby. I made an offer on it, and I'm making a deal with Mr. Marshall, the current owner. He lives over that hill and likes me well enough to want me for a neighbor. He's asking eleven thousand dollars for the thousand acres. I've given him a down payment of ten percent, and he'll take the rest when I can get it together. It will take a while before it's mine, but I'm telling, it will be and I'm going to build a dairy." The rush of words made Abijah feel as though he'd run a footrace and he hadn't even said the hard part yet.

"Well, you've certainly thought it through." Abby patted his arm.

"I was hoping, Abby, that you'd like it so much m...m-maybe you'd agree to live here with me someday. That is, will you marry me, Abby? Will you be my wife?" He hadn't thought what he would do if she said no.

Time stopped and Abijah dared not breathe as he awaited his fate. Finally, Abby answered. "Yes, I will, Abijah! I will be your wife." And Abijah saw the light in her eyes and a rare full smile on her face.

Then he presented her with the gift he'd been so anxious to give her. A necklace—heavy gold filigree links that hung nearly to Abby's waist. It was elaborate and looked out of place on her. She didn't say a word but as soon as he saw it and her expression, Abijah knew he'd made a mistake.

"Oh, this will not do. I'm sorry, Abby. I had thought to give you a fine gift but this just isn't right."

"I thank you for thinking of me, but if I were to wear it, I'd feel like I had all the California gold hanging off of me." She laughed a bit at this and Abijah felt himself relax.

"Would you prefer something else, Abby?"

"I would like to mark this occasion, because it is important to me. But I think a simple brooch would suffice, don't you?"

"There will be quite a bit of gold left over, what would you have me do with it?"

"I think you should put it toward your property, Abijah."

"You are a very practical woman, Abby."

"Yes, I am."

Abby unpacked picnic basket and they ate lunch on a horse blanket and enjoyed the warm sun and the cool breeze that reached them from Tomales Bay. He told her of his dream.

"Do you think it's possible, Abby? This place came to my dreams so long ago. I saw a smooth road with rolling hills. I sensed I was near a large body of water, but I couldn't quite see it. Just over a rise was a grove of trees and a driveway a mile long. It was flanked on either side with mature gum trees. The fragrant branches met overhead and created a rustling silvery-green tunnel. There were pastures of beautiful golden cows, some with white spots, and some were fawn-colored. It was milking time, and the mamas had lots of little calves following them, frolicking in the green fields. On the other side of the drive were two huge red barns with fenced paddocks. There was a big, white house at the end of the driveway and the sun glinted on the panes of glass in the windows. Standing outside the house was a man and a woman and three young men and two little girls. Abby, I think it was you and me with our children."

"Your dream makes me believe, Abijah. You paint a pretty picture, but I wonder where are all the trees you speak of? I don't see many."

"We're going to plant those trees. I saw that part, too. Can you imagine? Twelve thousand trees to form a windbreak and to hold the soil to the earth. I will plant them in the shapes of an anchor, a sailor with a sword, and the constellations—only the moon and the stars in the sky will see the shapes I've created. And I hope someday we'll have lots of children. I want that, Abby, do you?"

The far-away look in Abby's eyes vanished, and her expression became cold as she replied, "I will have two sons. And they will attend Harvard School of Law. They will be men of substance. And I'm not sure you should tell anyone else your ideas about anchors and dreams. Others might misunderstand you."

Her words cut. He believed that his dreams would be safe with her. He could not keep the disappointment from his voice. "Only my older brothers know about my dreams and now you, Abby." Had he made a grave mistake in telling her? He realized at that moment that in their partnership, he would be the dreamer, and she the pragmatic one. *Perhaps*, he thought, *there would be room for both*?

"Thank you for bringing me here and for telling me your thoughts, Abijah," she said, her voice softening.

"Thank you for listening to me, Abby," he replied. "I do agree, education is important. I wish I had more myself, but it's too late for me, I think. I read everything I can get my hands on to try to improve myself," he said earnestly. "Two sons aren't very many, though, and what if we have daughters? I wouldn't mind daughters. I love my sisters; they're some of my best friends."

"Two sons, Abijah, and that is the end of it. I will not have daughters. I will not raise girl children who cannot do what they wish with their lives. You know, women have very little power in and of themselves. A woman cannot even own property. It all must be done through the man. Why would I want to raise intelligent girls whose opportunities in life only come if they marry well?" The fire was back in her eyes, and he heard it in her voice and countered with his own argument.

"You've met my sisters; do they seem powerless? What about my mother? She is not weak in the least. She is much stronger than most men I know. I admire a strong woman. It's one of my favorite things about you, Abby. And, you are a teacher with a brilliant mind."

"And the minute we are wed, I will say goodbye to teaching other peoples' children. I will teach our sons until they are ready for high school, and I will help you in your endeavors." Abby replied as though she hadn't heard anything Abijah had said.

"I would never ask you to give up the things that make you happy, Abby."

"The success of our family will be my security, and I suppose I would call it my happiness. Quakers think differently about such things, you should know that if we are to be married. There is less emphasis on personal happiness and more focus on duty and loyalty and strong family bonds. That is what I want from you, Abijah. You and I have similar ideas about what we want in life. I think we will be a good match, and I will try my best to be a good wife."

Abijah didn't quite know what to say about her grim outlook on a woman's place in life, but he felt that everything could be agreed upon between them as they became better acquainted.

Cautiously, he rested his warm hand on her shoulder and pointed to where he'd build the barns, the house, and where they'd plant a forest of gum trees, redwoods, and cypress. The two were in very close proximity, but Abby did nothing to discourage the contact. She leaned into the shelter of his arms. The winds were fierce, but everything smelled so clean, and all dreams were possible when looked at from great heights.

Chapter Eleven
Mister and Missus

On December 26, 1864, they married at the Meecham Ranch near Petaluma, and Reverend James Wylie performed the ceremony. They were surrounded by family and a few close friends. Abby wore a grey silk dress and her grey Quaker's bonnet, and Abijah dressed in his Sunday best.

Unfortunately, it was also the night of one of the worst storms to hit the coast in the area's remembered history—hour upon hour of howling winds and icy rains so fierce that its strength changed the shape of the coastline. As they departed Petaluma, the young couple laughed that their married life was getting off to such an exciting start. They made it home safely to Tomales and slammed the front door of the makeshift shack against the torrential rain just as the worst of the storm hit.

When Abby came to live in Tomales with Abijah, he'd already been constructing outbuildings and raising livestock at the property for four years. Just before they married, he broke ground on what would be the smaller of two barns. The house he planned to build would have to wait until his dairy business began to pay off, but he knew it was just a matter of time and he was a patient man.

Abijah was not happy about the state of his home. It had been fine when he was a bachelor, but now he had a wife and she deserved more than an old sheep shack. Abby had assured him that she would be fine where they were until they had acquired enough money to build a proper home. She never complained but he knew she was not comfortable.

Several weeks after their wedding, the newlyweds received a letter from Chicago, Illinois. It was addressed to Mr. and Mrs. Abijah Woodworth, but Abijah didn't recognize the return address. He handed the letter to his wife.

"Do you know who this might be, Abby?"

Abby put down her knitting and held her hand out for the letter. "It's from my mother's brother, Diamond Jo Reynolds."

"That's quite a name. Is he Quaker?"

"He is. Everyone calls him Diamond Jo, but I've always just called him Uncle."

"And your mother?"

"She calls him Brother, or Joseph when they disagree."

"Open it! Anything sent by someone named Diamond Jo seems lucky to me."

Abby carefully opened the envelope, which contained a letter and a bank draft from her uncle. She began reading out loud:

> *To my dear niece, Abigail, and her husband, Abijah, I send you felicitations on your marriage and hope the day was everything you wished for. May you have both happiness and years of wise decisions—marriage is a partnership, after all. I hope you both find success in each other. Enclosed is a gift for your wedding—all the best, as ever, your Uncle Jo.*

"What did he send, Abby?" asked Abijah.

"He's given us a check for five thousand dollars," she said.

"That's a lot of money, Wife." he said, dumbfounded.

"We will put half the money in the bank, and the other half can go to building your barns. Uncle Jo would want some of the money to go towards your business, and I want it that way," she said, and she smiled as she looked at her husband.

"For once, I think I'm speechless." Now, Abijah knew he could afford to build proper barns for his cows.

Abijah walked up the road to his house with several letters. There was a thick envelope from his mother and something for Abby from her brother, Brad.

He poured himself some coffee that was kept warm on the stove and sat down to read. He wasn't sure where his wife was, but he wanted to get back to his cows before long. He opened the letter and read the first few lines.

Dearest Abijah, I am so sorry to tell you that our sweet Martha has gone to her reward, August 3, 1867. I'm sure it's a blessing, she has suffered so this last year...

Abijah stopped reading. *Where was Abby?* He felt tears gathering in the corners of his eyes as he thought of his sister. *She was such a kind woman and a patient mother to her children. What would the little ones do without her? And poor Isaac, he would be lost. He loved her so.*

"Abby!" he hollered. "Abby, where are you?" No answer.

Finally she came in. "What's wrong, Abijah?" She'd had been out in the vegetable garden picking squash for supper.

"Martha's gone. My sister is gone." Tears rolled down his cheeks.

"Oh, your poor mother. We must go be with her."

"Yes. You're right. We'll leave tomorrow afternoon?"

"I think we should, I'm so sorry Abijah. I know how fond of Martha you were. May I read your letter?"

He handed it to her. "Read it to me, please. I only got to a few lines before I stopped."

Abby read the rest of the letter to her husband. After a few minutes, he said, "I'm going out to the barn, time for the bossies." He wiped his face with his handkerchief and walked away, hat in hand and head down.

Once he'd had gone, she sat down and read the forgotten letter from Bradley—nothing much of importance, just weekly news of the family. Then she wrote to Martha's husband, Isaac Fuller, and extended their sincere condolences and informed him they'd be there for the funeral.

Abby got supper in the oven. She suspected Abijah wouldn't have an appetite, but he had to keep up his strength. She would make him eat if she had to. After dinner, she decided to bake a cake to bring to his parents house and went through her supplies to make sure she had everything she needed. Then she went to their bedroom and packed a valise for them both. By the time she'd finished, Abijah was due to come in from the barn. She set the table and waited for him.

Finally, he came back and washed up at the kitchen sink. "Sit down and eat. Everything's ready for you." Abijah didn't say anything as he waited for her to join him. They ate silently.

Abijah put his fork down. "Abby, I'll ask the neighbors to look out for our animals while were gone. We'll go first thing in the morning." He seemed to be mulling over everything over he needed to attend to before they could leave for Stony Point.

Abby nodded in agreement. "I'm making a cake tonight for your mother. And I wrote to Isaac, maybe you'd like to add a few lines."

"Thank you. I'll do that now. Then I think I'll go to bed if you don't mind. This day's taken it out of me." He spoke with effort as he added his own message to Abby's letter, then shook his head sadly. "There aren't adequate words to convey my sorrow. I never know what to say at these times."

"No one does. We carry on and we try our best and that is all we can do. You rest now, Husband. Tomorrow will come early and you'll need your strength." Abby kissed his cheek.

Martha had a weak heart and lungs, and ultimately succumbed to pneumonia. She was a 35-year-old wife and mother, and five years senior to Abijah.

Most of Abijah's family had already assembled and was waiting for them when they arrived. It was a sad event, but the Woodworth's had always been stronger together and it was truer now than ever.

Abby was amazed at how gracious Marilla was. She greeted everyone with a smile and kind words. "Hello," she said in a soft voice. "Thank you for coming."

"Of course, we came," Abby said, and was startled when Marilla grabbed her and hugged tight.

"My heart is breaking for my darling daughter." Abby shook her head, she was sure Marilla hadn't slept since the tragic news. She worried that the older woman would make herself ill.

Parmenus was also uncharacteristically quiet, but seemed pleased to be in the presence of his loved ones. Abby never really knew what to think of Abijah's father. He rarely spoke with her and she knew he didn't care for the Quaker religion. She wasn't even sure that he liked her—not that it mattered much to her.

They'd been at Stony Point just an hour when Isaac Fuller arrived with his children. There was a hush when his buggy pulled up to the house. Isaac got down and helped the girls out and the boys jumped out after. They all looked like they could do with a good meal.

Abby went to the kitchen to see if anything could be put together quickly for the grieving family to eat. She didn't want to make them wait until supper time. She needn't have worried, as every surface was filled with covered dishes. The neighbors had been busy, making sure that Marilla didn't have to do any cooking. There was a sink full of dishes though, so Abby found an apron and pushed up her sleeves and got to work. Her husband found her drying the dishes and trying to figure out where to put them away.

"You don't have to do that, Abby. But thank you, anyhow. I know my mother appreciates it."

"I don't want her to have to do it and honestly, I'm better off in the kitchen. I feel so out of place." She put the last dish away, laid the damp towel over the edge of the sink and removed her apron.

"You aren't out of place, but I understand. These are hard times." Abijah grabbed both of her hands for a moment and gave them a squeeze.

"Will you ask your mother if I can get this food out to the dining room? People should eat, if they can. Especially the children, I think."

"You're right. I'll be back."

Abijah returned right away and helped Abby load the table with food, plates, and utensils. A few people helped themselves and the children ate, mostly cakes and breads, but at least they had something.

Isaac sat next to Marilla. He hadn't said much since he'd arrived. Abby asked if he'd like her to fix him a plate, but he said he couldn't eat. After about an hour, he went to the room that Marilla had prepared for him, closed the door, and that was the last anyone saw of him that night.

The entire family was staying with Marilla and Parmenus until the funeral and the house was filled. It had been a long time since they'd all been together, so although it was a sad occasion, they all enjoyed one another's company. During the day, Abijah helped his pa and his brothers with the farm work and Abby helped out in the kitchen and made sure that Marilla was taken care of. After supper, there were games of checkers or chess, and quiet conversations.

Abijah took every moment he could to commune with nature. When he walked the boundaries of his property, he felt as though he was in church. He hoped to share that feeling with his wife.

"Join me for walk, would you Abby?" Abijah asked hopefully.

"I need to finish the mending," she replied.

He wondered sometimes if she thought he was lazy, always stopping to go for a walk. He wasn't. He was up before the roosters each morning. He just knew that he needed a break sometimes. Especially since Martha's passing, he needed time to count his blessings.

"I won't mind if you'll promise to come with me next time," he said.

Abby was just too disciplined. He knew she had a lot to do around the property, they both did. *But a person needed to take time and appreciate what he had once in a while.* As soon as he could afford it, he resolved to get Abby some help—whether she wanted it or not.

"I will, Abijah." Abby didn't look up from her sewing.

Abijah surveyed his land and thought of all he had accomplished—Woodworth land. There he stood near the top of the hill and breathed deeply. He contemplated his hard-won fortunes and daydreamed of the turning seasons.

He marveled at the renewal of life brought by spring rains when the sun's soft rays reached through the fog and mist-laden mornings. He loved the golden hills as they shimmered in the summer heat, and the cloud of fine dust that seemed to settle into everything. Autumn months were for the harvest and working together for the common good of the community. Winter signaled long hours of darkness, the march of time, and roaring fires as the family gathered at the hearth.

Chilling winds off the bay made for bracing mornings, and the buffeting shaped the coast and trees and everything in its way. But, just as stones were worn down by rushing water, Mother Nature created the land as she pleased.

He turned away from the magical vista and hiked back to the house where Abby waited for him. What could possibly make his world even more perfect? Perhaps soon his wife would give him news of a child.

As newlyweds, Abby and Abijah settled quickly into a companionable marriage. Abijah worked hard getting the dairy started, taking care of the animals, building the barns, and finally completing the beautiful farmhouse he designed. For Abby's part, she helped him in whatever ways she could, even helping him build the grape-stake fences that marked their property. Each day, they worked side by side, and their labors didn't seem quite as difficult when they shared the burdens with one another.

Abijah watched his wife as she hung off the edge of the cliff in order to secure a section of the fencing. He whistled into the wind, she was strong and determined. She really was a perfect match. "Abby, you sure you're okay? It's a mighty long drop."

"I think I'm alright as long as you don't say things like that and as long as there's something I can be tied to."

"It's a good thing we're young and strong. I can't imagine someone Mr. Marshall's age having to fix these danged fences."

"I simply will not look down." Abby gave a forced little laugh.

From the beginning, they discussed the day-to-day workings of the ranch. Abijah shared all business matters with his wife and relied upon her understanding of the business.

People commented what a good match they'd made, and Abby didn't mind too much that everyone kept asking when the two were planning to start their family. She always answered, "Do you see the work we still have to get this place in order? No children yet, I hope. We've got too much to do."

It was becoming more difficult for her to rise from bed each day and Abby was terribly unhappy about being at the whims of a body she no longer seemed to be able to control. "*I cannot see my feet!*" she yelled out the bedroom door and shook her head in disgust. Then the little invader gave her a good swift kick.

She heard a crash and a "*Hot damn!*" Abijah was trying to be of help in the kitchen.

He was cooking again. "Here, you sit down, I'll finish up." Abijah gave her a sigh and sat at the kitchen table with his coffee.

"How are you f..feeling, Abby?"

She took stock of herself before answering. "I am fine." She looked down and rubbed at where the baby had just kicked. "To be perfectly honest, I am growing bigger each day and I am weary of this condition I find myself in." She chuckled and looked at her Abijah.

He patted her shoulder exactly the way he treated one of his milk cows. "I think you look beautiful, Abby. You are aglow." She snorted in reply and served up their porridge.

"I am not glowing. I am sweating with exertion brought on by this enormous baby in me. Your fault, entirely, by the way." Her voice was harsh, but then she looked over at her husband and smiled at him. She was hungry but after a few mouthfuls of porridge she no longer had an appetite. Instead, she sipped at her tea while her husband ate with gusto.

"Well, I think you are lovely and by my reckoning we're going to have a baby any day now."

"If you say so." She mocked him, but truthfully, he had more experience with babies, than she did. To be precise, she had no experience with childbirth or babies. Abijah had seen his younger sister and brother born, and assisted with countless livestock births. Abby felt momentarily nauseated as she continued to fret. It was impossible to imagine something so enormous coming out of her. It didn't seem physically possible. Abijah knew of her worries and had tried to allay her fears. She'd just have to trust him.

"I do say so. I've sent word to Ma and she'll be here tomorrow or the next day. Can you wait, little baby?" He had leaned toward the belly and spoke.

"I suppose we must. But you could probably do just as well, couldn't you, Abijah?"

"Oh, I'm sure I could. But I think it best if Ma's here."

On July 17, 1869, more than five years after they wed, Abby gave birth to a healthy son, Frederick. Marilla and Abijah were both with Abby and the birth went as well as they could have hoped for.

"Abby, next time it will go faster, I promise." Marilla assured her with a soft voice, and Abby groaned in discomfort.

Abijah stared down at his wife and son. "You did really well, Abby. Our son is perfect. Big lad. Give him to me for a moment." He reached down for the baby and smiled at his wife. She was exhausted with good reason. The birth had gone on longer than it should have and Abijah was beginning to worry when the baby finally made his appearance. "Rest, little mother. I'll hold the wee lad for a while." Abby closed her eyes.

Abby might have known a lot about school-aged children, but she knew next to nothing about babies and toddlers. The constant care for something utterly helpless in the world had been a bit of a shock to her. She felt she should be doing so many things, but instead, she was obligated to take care of a tiny human who couldn't do for himself.

It was Abijah that knew more about the little ones. Their care didn't intimidate him and he was always happy to lend a hand when he could. He loved babies and little children, and found his wife's surprise somewhat amusing.

"Abijah, I admit the appeal of these tiny creatures may be lost on me. They're so dependent. And so greedy," Abby said with a rueful smile. She was up before dawn, nursing Fred at the kitchen table. Her husband sat with her for a few moments before getting back to work.

"That may be true, but look how he trusts you. You are his world, Abby. He's a handsome lad."

Two years later, Ralph was born. "Thank heavens he's not so big as his brother. Really, Abijah, I had no business having a baby as big as

Fred, he's a lot to lift. But this one, I can tell he's an easier size to handle."

Abby looked down at Ralph and tried to see him in the same way her husband saw him, but she could not. Where Abijah saw sweetness, Abby saw only dirty diapers, feedings that interrupted desperately needed sleep, and a child that would be years before he could care of himself. Of course, she had motherly feelings for both boys, but those feelings did not negate all the work that little ones required. Her sons were strong and handsome, though, and Abby was pleased; she had fulfilled her promise to Abijah.

Being a mother left her lonely much of the time, and she felt a separation from her husband she was not prepared for. Abijah had the ranch hands to talk to, and his brothers were always stopping by to work or visit. But she only had the company of the babies.

Abby didn't consider childrearing to be sufficient stimulation and worried at its toll on her mental faculties. Her experience with maternal duty was not quite what she'd expected, and if she were being honest, the long days spent home alone with children underfoot was quite a nuisance. Someday, her boys would be young men and make her a proud mother, but unfortunately, it would be years before that came to pass.

Abijah's parents were coming to visit tomorrow. They hadn't been to Tomales since Ralph's birth and Abby was eager to have her mother-in-law visit. She was very fond of Marilla and always wished her own mother was as pleasant. But the idea of entertaining Parmenus for several days made her head ache. Of course, Abijah's father would be outdoors with his son most of the time, but still. He made her uncomfortable.

"Your father doesn't like me much, Abijah." Abby mentioned during supper.

"What would make you say that?" His brow furrowed in thought.

"He's never done or said a thing to me, but I feel his disapproval as strong as can be." She got up to make tea and Abijah followed her into the kitchen. "I worry he'll find fault with me." There had been times when she felt as though at any moment he might begin to shout fire and brimstone at her or worse, he might start on about her Quaker faith.

"My father believes you and I make a very good match. Have you ever thought about how he might feel about my lack of religion?"

"No. I guess I haven't."

"We argued a bit at first, he wanted to understand my position. But he never disrespected me for having different views. He's actually a very accepting man once you get to know him. And you will, get to know him, Abby. It would make me happy."

This was not the first time her husband had surprised her with his insights. She may have been more educated then he, but Abijah Woodworth understood human nature in ways that she simply could not. "I will try, Abijah. In New York, I was surrounded by the Quaker faith. It was my life. Here in California, I feel that I am only still Quaker because I say I am. My brothers, I fear are the same. We are Quaker only in name."

"Abby, your faith is being tested. You'll be just fine." He patted her hand.

Ralphie woke up crying. Abby gathered him in her arms, soothing him, and pretty soon, he gave a little hiccup and fell back asleep. Fred was still napping and Abby took the opportunity to get herself washed up.

Abijah had pumped water for her and she had it on the stove to heat. She dragged the tin tub into the kitchen and checked to make sure the water had heated enough. It was scalding. She poured in the two pots, and then tempered the water with two more buckets of cool. Now all that remained was for her to get in and washed up before those babies woke up.

She'd just rinsed the soap out of her hair and when Ralphie started crying. She stood up and got herself wrapped up in flannel and ran to the bedroom. The baby was in his crib and Freddie was on their bed, still asleep and supported with bolsters so he wouldn't roll off. Abby let the baby cry while she got dressed and she'd just got her boots buttoned when Abijah slammed the back door which set off another round of wails from the crib. Now Freddie was awake too. She heard her husband dragging the tub of water into the mudroom.

Abby took Freddie's hand and propelled him into the kitchen while holding onto the crying baby. She lifted the older boy into his high-chair and the muscles in her back protested, but she ignored her aching body.

"Abijah, I'm heating more water to add to your bath. It's going to take a few minutes."

She thought she heard him, but now both children were crying and she couldn't be positive.

"Here's a cup of milk, Freddie. I'm going to feed Ralphie and then you can have your dinner." But first, she heated more water on the stove.

Her oldest son was appeased but not for long. Still nursing the baby, Abby fixed Freddie a bowl of mash potatoes and green beans. She set it in front of him and watched him feed himself with a spoon. He managed to get as much of it plastered in his dark hair as he got in his mouth. In the meantime, she burped Ralphie and he was nodding off again, so she set him down in the little basket she kept for him in the kitchen. Now, she could get Freddie cleaned up. "Get down, get down," he said over and over.

"Abijah, your water's ready. Do you want me to bring it?" She waited but he didn't answer so she brought the pails of water into the other room and there was her husband asleep in the luke warm water. "I'm pouring more water in." He woke with as start. "Hot water's coming."

"Thank you, Abby." She added more and more until finally the hot water had all been added. In the other room she could hear the children and left her husband to bathe. Her hair was still dripping, hanging down her aching back. She had so much to do to prepare before Abijah's parents arrived.

The first thing Marilla noticed were the dark circles under Abby's eyes. "You're not getting enough rest," she announced.

"I'll be fine, Mother. The children keep me very busy but they mostly sleep through the night."

"Has your mother been here to help you?"

"She has not. And if she did come, I'd not only have the boys and Abijah to tend to, but I'd have her as well. My mother requires a lot of attention. I am much better off without her help."

Marilla remembered how exhausting new babies could be. When she was a new mother, she had help from her mother.

"Abby, may I stay and help you? Parmenus will go back to Stony Point on Sunday. He has work to do but I could stay here to help out." She watched Abby and saw the rigid line of her back relax almost imperceptibly in acquiescence.

"We'd be most appreciative." Marilla watched as Abby smiled for the first time in a very long time.

"Abby, what do you mean, no more children? The boys are young; maybe they'd like a little brother or sister to play with." They were sitting up in bed; Abby was reading business papers sent by her brother while Abijah read the newspaper. At his remark she put the papers down and turned to her husband with a scowl on her face.

"How many times are you going to bring this up?"

"Alright, I understand, no more children. But a man is entitled to enjoy the pleasures of the marital bed. It's in the Bible." The moment it was out of his mouth, he knew he'd gone wrong.

"Don't you dare attempt to quote scripture to me, Mr. Woodworth. Of all people, you should understand that pleasures of the marital bed are what lead to more children."

"Not always, Abby. Not always. We could be more careful." Maybe he should have backed down. But he didn't.

"That's no guarantee, and you know it."

There was no point arguing but he proceed against his better judgment. "What am I supposed to do, Abby, if I cannot lie with you?"

"This was our agreement. Are you going back on your word?"

Abijah shook his head, but didn't comment further.

She would have the last word. "I stuck to my word and gave you two sons. Tomorrow's Monday, wash day. I need my rest." With that, she turned over on her side and ended the argument.

And that was the end of the matter. For a while.

Chapter Twelve
The Widow

It was quite by accident that Abijah met Mrs. Williams. He was on his way into town when he noticed her walking along the road in the same direction. It was a hot day, and Abijah offered her a ride.

"That would be most appreciated, Sir."

"Allow me to introduce m...m-myself. Abijah Woodworth, at your service." He tipped his hat and then leaped down to help the lady into his wagon.

"I'm Lisbeth Williams."

"Very pleased to meet you. I heard about your husband, Ma'am. My deepest sympathies for your loss."

"Thank you. Yes, things have not been easy since I lost my Trevor. You must think I'm daft for walking in this heat. My horse needs shoeing, and I don't want to ride until that's taken care of. When I left the house, it seemed pleasant enough. Strange really, since it's usually windy and damp and cold in these parts."

"I'd be happy to get your horse fixed up. It wouldn't take long, but I'd have to do it tomorrow. I've got business in town, and then I need to get back home and see to my animals."

"Your help would be welcomed."

"My pleasure, of course."

When they arrived in town, Abijah got down and helped the widow out of the wagon. He noticed she smelled like flowers.

"My business will take about an hour if you'd like a ride home?"

"If you don't mind, I'd be delighted. I need a few things at the mercantile, and I hope to see my attorney. I'll be done and ready whenever you are."

Lisbeth Williams walked across the road and headed toward a small house that belonged to the solicitor. Abijah made his way to the mercantile. When he went into the store, he was greeted by a group of ladies. They were visiting while they waited for their weekly orders to be completed. Abijah tipped his hat to the group.

"Good afternoon, Mr. Woodworth," said a pretty young lady with auburn hair and a blue calico dress.

"I see you've met Mrs. Williams," the shopkeeper's wife said in disapproving tones.

"That I have," said Abijah. Already feeling guilty, he was unwilling to say more about the widow. He turned his attention to his supply list but felt several pairs of eyes boring into his back, like an ant under a magnifying glass in the sun. Abijah already accepted the fact that he'd just become their new source of gossip. *Damn it.* He had to get home and explain to his wife. If she heard this from someone else first, he'd never be forgiven, and he knew the news from the village was both speedy and ruthless. He'd seen reputations ruined in a single afternoon.

The shopkeeper, Mr. Smith, an older man with white hair and drooping mustache, came out of the back room. "'Bije, good to see you. What can I get you today?"

"Just a few things. The usual." He said and handed over his list of provisions. "I was wondering if you had any new reading materials come in? I want to get a little something for the missus."

"Have a look while I get your order together." Mr. Smith placed a box of books on the counter for Abijah to peruse.

After a few minutes, he selected a book Abby was sure to enjoy. *Excursions* by Henry David Thoreau. He paged carefully through the book and loved the quiet beauty of Thoreau's words and apt descriptions. Abijah thought he would like very much to visit the places the author wrote about, and imagined Abby and himself reading the chapters together on cold nights in front of the fire.

Mr. Smith broke Abijah's reverie. "The order's ready, and I see you found a book. Shall I add that to your account?" Abijah nodded and waved goodbye.

It didn't take long to load the wagon with provisions, and while he waited for Mrs. Williams to finish up in the store, Abijah read more of Thoreau.

Fred and Ralph were in their room doing their schoolwork, and Abijah took the opportunity to tell his wife about his afternoon in town.

"I gave Mrs. Williams a ride to the mercantile today," he said casually.

"Huh. How did you know she needed a ride?" Abby was washing dishes after their evening meal.

The Secret Lives of Ancestors

"I didn't. But I saw her walking on the road to town, so I stopped to see if I could help her."

Now he had her full attention. "Why was she walking?"

"Her horse is in need of a farrier. I offered to do that for her tomorrow if you don't mind. Won't take me long and I thought you could come with me. She might be nice company for you."

"Perhaps another time. I've got canning to finish." Abby dried the dishes and stacked them on the kitchen table. "How is she keeping since her husband's passing?"

"She mentioned things had been difficult. I don't think she's accustomed to making decisions on her own."

"Well, I've never met her, but of course, the ladies in town keep me up-to-date about all that's going on." *They sure did*, thought Abijah.

"I brought you something, Abby." He placed the book in her hands.

"That was thoughtful. I'm ready for something new to read." She opened the cover and ran her hands carefully over the title page. "Thank you."

"I was hoping we could read it together. I glanced through a few pages, and I'm very interested in this author's writing."

"As you wish. We'll begin tonight," she said.

The next day after he'd finished tending to his animals, Abijah drove down the hill to the widow's property. Mrs. Williams came out of the house as he pulled up and waved to him. She was wearing a yellow dress with a smudged white apron. Her strawberry blond hair was up in a loose bun that drooped charmingly to one side.

"Greetings, Mr. Woodworth," she called from the front porch.

"Hello there, Mrs. Williams!"

"I appreciate your help. The barn is behind the house to the left."

"I'll find everything, don't worry. This won't take long."

"Come up to the house for refreshments when you're finished," she called out.

After the first visit, Abijah found excuses to visit the Williams property a few times a month–a broken wheel, an escaped ram. Abby never went with him when he paid his calls, although he always invited her. She was much too busy to go along. Eventually, he stopped asking and began arranging his week around those visits down the hill.

Lisbeth, as he'd come to think of her, baked on the days Abijah would visit. He would do some little chore for her, and then she'd invite him for a visit with a cup of tea and dessert. How could he refuse?

Abijah was smitten with the young widow. He thought about her all day as he worked. He wondered if she was thinking about him the same way. He knew it was wrong for him to think about another woman, but he couldn't seem to resist her. She was beautiful and lonely, and she smelled like springtime. If Abby noticed anything strange or untoward, she made no mention.

The day was windy and rainy. The sky was dark, and a storm was coming. He arrived at the Williams property, waved at Lisbeth standing in the doorway, and drove his wagon around to the barn. He wanted to check on the repairs he'd made to the roof to make sure it would hold up in the storm.

After he'd been there a few minutes, she came into the barn, hair mussed, shawl, and dress soaking wet. "Can you stop up at the house for a visit before you leave, Abijah?"

"I'm nearly finished. I wanted to make sure the repairs will hold. Looks just fine so I'll go back with you."

Abijah put his arm around Lisbeth and they made a mad dash through the rain. In her mudroom, she helped Abijah out of his coat and hat. She removed her wet shawl.

"You're soaked through. Stay in the kitchen where it's warm. I'm going to get us some blankets and put the kettle on. It won't take a minute," she said quickly.

Abijah moved into the kitchen, still dripping wet. He paced the floor, trying to decide what to do. She was lonely and desirable and very kind. He waited for her. His foolish mind made up.

The Woodworth's took the wagon into town for their weekly supplies. Abby needed fabric for new shirts for the boys and Abijah, and she hoped to find something with which to make herself a new dress. When they arrived, they were greeted by the town gossips, couldn't wait to hear the latest and to tell all they knew, too.

"Hello, Mrs. Woodworth, Mr. Woodworth. How are things?" asked one of the ladies.

The Secret Lives of Ancestors

"We are fine, thank you. And how are you?" Abby greeted them and Abijah waved and waited at the counter for the shopkeeper.

"Oh, I'm just fine. I was speaking with my friends about one of our newer neighbors. Perhaps you've met the Widow Williams, Mrs. Woodworth. She moved here last year with her husband and tragically he died unexpectedly shortly after they'd arrived. Anyway, I expect you must have met her since we see Mr. Woodworth turning his wagon onto the road she lives on quite frequently," the woman said smugly.

"I haven't had the time to meet Mrs. Williams. I'm very busy with the ranch, but please understand that I know who she is, and my husband is doing his duty as a member of this community to help her in her time of need. Her late husband left the property in disarray, and Abijah is making much-needed repairs."

Inside, Abby was seething with anger and hurt, but she'd never let those awful ladies know. Abijah waited for her outside. He'd left the moment the conversation turned toward the Widow. He could feel that he was in for a long, unpleasant discussion with his wife.

"Abijah, people are talking about you going to the Williams property. Are you still visiting her?"

"I go there occasionally to do a few chores to help her out. I have invited you to join me many times, but you're always too busy."

"Well, maybe you shouldn't go there anymore. We have become the source of public discussion."

"If you would prefer that I not help out Mrs. Williams, then I will not."

Abijah sat in the kitchen while Abby cut up apples for the pies she was making. He was overcome with guilt about his affair with the Widow. It had been just twice, but he was sick with worry. If his pa and ma were still living, they'd be dishonored by his behavior. This thought made him feel even lower. He had to extricate himself from this terrible situation.

He drank his tea in silence and pondered the misery that his life had become.

"I thought we'd pay a visit to Mrs. Williams," Abby said. "You don't think a surprise visit will bother her do you?" Abijah shook his head, eyes wide.

"I think it is the best way to stop the rumors, don't you?"

Abijah nearly choked on his drink. "I'm sure she'd be very pleased to meet you. When did you think you'd like to go?" He answered reasonably, but inside he was shaken. His apprehension came with good reason.

"Why don't we go today? I'm nearly finished here. I shall I bring some her some blackberry jam."

"T...t-Today, is soon. But alright, I think that would be very n...n-nice—the j...j-jam, that is. And the visit." He looked at Abby and saw her eyes narrowed.

"Then I'll just finish up here, Abijah."

"I'll bring the wagon around," he said, the feeling of dread pressing down on him with cruel hands.

Abby presented a little basket with jars of blackberry jam to Mrs. Williams. At first the woman looked utterly surprised to see the Woodworth's at her front door.

"Oh Abby, thank you." Mrs. Williams recovered and grasped Abby's hand in her two hands. "I'm so happy to meet you. I've been asking Abijah to bring you around for months. I don't have any female companionship here." Abby was highly unsettled with the familiarity Mrs. Williams displayed. And when she'd grabbed at her, Abby narrowed her eyes and winced. She didn't enjoy being handled, particularly by strangers. And the way the woman spoke of Abijah was unacceptable.

"Mrs. Williams, it's nice to meet you. My husband and I thought it was high time we were introduced," Abby said.

Abijah was becoming more alarmed by the minute. The look on Abby's face would have been inscrutable to a stranger, but he saw plainly that trouble was brewing. He felt strongly that if he didn't get her away from Lisbeth immediately and back home to safety, he was doomed.

Lisbeth offered tea. He declined, hoping to keep their visit as short as possible, but to his dismay, Abby agreed. Thirty minutes of excruciating small talk and Abijah was sure his heart was going to give out. They sat stiffly in the kitchen, speaking of weather, Tomales, Mr. Williams' passing, the repairs that Abijah had made in the barn. Conversation was stilted and fraught with tension. Abijah watched Abby carefully and saw her give a slight nod as if she had decided something. And then his wife set her cup down.

"My husband and I shall take our leave. Thank you for the tea."

Abby got up from the table and Lisbeth stood with a puzzled look that turned quickly to a knowing expression of horror. Abby walked to the front door, opened it, and left the house. She got into the wagon without waiting for Abijah's assistance.

The Secret Lives of Ancestors

Abijah was right behind her. He was stunned by her behavior and what it implied. She knew. Somehow, over a handshake and a cup of tea, she'd figured it out. But how?

As soon as they were out of earshot, she let him have it. "You were unfaithful to me with that woman." Abby didn't ask; she *told* him how it was in a low, harsh voice.

There was no point lying about it. "Abby, I'm s...s-sorry," he said. He knew these empty words could not repair the damage he'd done to his marriage.

"How could you do this to me? I trusted you. Did you think me too stupid to realize what was happening under my nose? I guess I'd expect it of a man, but how could a woman do such a terrible thing to another woman? I'll be the talk of the town." Abijah took one look at his wife's distraught face. His wife was as close to tears as he'd ever seen her and he knew he'd done a terrible wrong.

Abby wrote to her brother, Ike, that very night to tell him of Abijah's infidelity. He wrote back and suggested she visit him, and he'd help her figure things out.

Upon reading his reply, she informed her husband. "I'm going to San Francisco to visit Ike."

"When will you come back, Abby?" He asked so pathetically. Where had her strong husband disappeared to? She watched his heartbroken face as he awaited his fate. *Good. I hope you suffer.*

"I am undecided. But you better believe I'll be back, and there will be a solution to this trouble you've caused our family."

"Are...Are Fred and Ralph coming with you?" he asked. Sheepishly thinking how much he'd miss his young sons while they were gone.

"Certainly not. You will take care of them, and we'll see how you fare being in charge of an eight-year-old and a six-year-old. I suspect they will keep you busy and out of trouble while I am gone."

And with that, she hitched the horse to the buggy and made her way quickly down the driveway.

Abby returned two weeks later, quiet and uncommunicative but considerably more settled than when she'd left the ranch. Abijah hoped that with time, she would forgive him. He prayed that eventually, he could earn her trust once again.

It was no coincidence the Widow Williams decided Tomales was quite inhospitable and couldn't tolerate the hard stares given her by its townsfolk. She arranged for her solicitor to sell her property and got on a train heading to the East Coast. If anyone from Tomales heard from her again, it was never disclosed.

Chapter Thirteen
Forgiveness

The evening was damp, and the howling wind tried its best to lift the shingles from the roof. Winter nights, especially when the moon was new, always felt so long and lonely. The boys were already in bed when their father came in from milking his cows. The hired men had been fed and gone to their bunkhouse. Abijah had duties in the barns before he could call it a night.

Abby heard the back door slam. Her husband was finally home from tending his cows.

"My hands need a good soaking. I'm afraid they're 'bout frozen." Abijah began the process of peeling off his outer clothing and hanging it on hooks in the mudroom. He came to the kitchen in his stocking feet, but still wearing heavy work pants with his long underwear underneath.

"Sit down here and let me get a good look at your hands, Abijah." Abby checked his hands for untended cuts and possible infection but only saw dirt, calluses, and swollen joints. She got a big bowl and filled it with hot water, soap, and a dash of Sloan's Horse Liniment for good measure. The horse medicine worked wonders on achy muscles, but it stunk up the whole kitchen, and the vapors made the eyes water.

"Take your ease and get a good soak." Abby draped a rough towel over his shoulder and turned back to the woodstove and the pot of stew she had kept warm.

Abijah submerged his aching hands into the bowl and gave a soft moan, part pain from the medicated water and part relief from the soothing heat.

"You could use a good face washing, get it done so I can serve your dinner."

"Let me be for just a minute; my hands are bad tonight. Those dear old bossies got the best of me today."

"Here, I'll do it. Hold still and close your eyes. Whew, that liniment is strong." She took the towel and wet it in the wash water. Ringing out most of the water, she scrubbed at the back of his neck and ears and then went to work on the rest of his face.

"Abby, careful. Are you trying to sand me like a block of wood?" he joked wearily. "You're too good to me, girl."

"I am no girl, and you know it. It is my duty to help thee. That was our agreement."

"Oh, I thought you were being the kind wife to me."

"It is no kindness; it is duty." She removed the bowl and dirty wash water and began serving him at the kitchen table. She slammed a tin of biscuits down and a plate of soft butter, and a jar filled with honey. Next, she ladled up a bowl with hearty beef stew and set it down in front of her husband. She was about to turn away and begin the kitchen chores when Abijah laid his hand on her arm.

"Will you sit with me while I eat supper? Maybe you'd like one of these biscuits?" He handed her one he'd already smeared with butter and honey. Abby took it but said nothing, just sat eating quietly and watching her husband carefully.

"I was about starving, but you made a meal fit for a king." He tucked in and didn't stop until his bowl was empty. Abby automatically got up to get him more stew.

"There's only half a bowl left. Men ate a lot tonight. You must have worked them hard."

"Half's all I need."

Now he ate more slowly and watched his wife as she resumed her nibbling at her biscuit.

"Abby, it's been more than a year, do you ever think you could see your way clear to forgiving me?" he asked. His wife said nothing for a long time. He continued taking slow spoonfuls of the stew until he'd emptied his bowl.

She opened her mouth as if to say something and then closed it tight and gave her head a little shake.

"I surely miss those days when we were such good friends and partners. Those were heavenly days for us, Abby. I miss our walks in the hills. I miss telling you my dreams and you telling me yours."

"'Tis your own fault those days came to an end. Now, leave me to the kitchen. Get your rest, Husband. Milking time comes early." She put the dishes in the sink and began washing them with the remaining hot water in the kettle. The stew was gone; not one spoonful was left. Abijah scraped his chair when he got up from the table.

"Goodnight, Mrs. Woodworth," he said tiredly and made his way slowly to their bedroom.

Abby stayed longer in the kitchen than she needed to. She thought a long time about forgiveness. Could she do it? Would she ever trust him again? *I don't know. I suppose I could forgive, but I'm not sure I can ever trust again. What good would it do me?*

She may not have said she'd forgiven her husband, but she did thaw out a bit. Abijah felt it and was grateful they began to move forward in a sort of truce. One thing Abby and Abijah were in agreement about were their children. Both wanted the boys to have advantages they themselves had been denied.

They had very different parenting styles but it seemed to work for their family. Abby was aware that most men didn't give their roles in the children's lives much thought. But Abijah was very involved and seemed to count on being part of his sons' daily lives. Abby found she quite appreciated it and enjoyed when the four of them did things as a family.

She was very strict, while Abijah didn't feel much need to discipline his boys. He believed that if they were taught properly to begin with, they would most always make the right choices. After all, he and his siblings had done just fine—all Woodworth children were upstanding citizens. Abby rolled her eyes when her husband shared this bit of wisdom—she knew that children needed constant guidance.

Fred and Ralph spent their summers camping in the ever expanding forest their father had planted. Although not far from the house, the boys felt as though they were alone and liked the independent feeling it gave them. They were unaware that Abijah checked on their safety. He watched unnoticed as his sons worked together to make their fire, set up their tent, and prepared hot tea before retiring to their bedrolls.

Occasionally, Abijah would announce that he was taking a few hours off work, and the family would take the wagon down to Dillon Beach for a picnic. The boys and their father ran and played in the surf while Abby watched them from the sandy shore. She marveled that her husband had the energy to enjoy himself so thoroughly. Almost like having three boys, she chuckled to herself. After staying in the cold water as long as they could stand it, the three made their way back, with teeth chattering but happy smiles on their faces. The salt air and wind off the water created powerful appetites, and food always tasted better at the beach. After lunch, the boys ran off to explore tide pools until it was time to get back home.

In winter, Fred and Ralph sat at the windows in the parlor and daydreamed while watching the wind that blew off the coast make the trees sway wildly and the house timbers creak. Some days they raced each other around in the ballroom and slid in their stocking feet on the polished wood floors or played hide and seek in the closets and hallways.

"Listen to our boys, Abby. They sound like wild things hooting and hollering!" Abijah was pleasantly surprised his wife allowed such carrying on in the house.

"They're taking a break from geography class. Children need that, you know," she said.

Abby taught the boys at home, and they were receiving an excellent education. She kept them on an aggressive academic schedule yet allowed plenty of time for recess and lunch breaks. As a former teacher, she knew her boys needed fresh air and movement, or they'd never sit still to learn. After their lessons, they helped their father in the barn until dinner time. After dinner, they did their homework until bedtime.

Abby managed to keep the boys from getting restless during the school day by finding things specific to each child that would allow them to explore their creative side. Fred was very boisterous and competitive. Whether it was hiking, debating, or practicing arithmetic, he had to be first, or he'd become very frustrated with himself and unpleasant to be around. Ralph was quieter and preferred music and painting and quiet exploration of the natural world. He was always excited to attend the births of the various animals on the ranch, while Fred showed very little interest. Ralph was dogged in his research and was the better student, but he didn't seem to need to win all the time. He appeared satisfied when Fred won any competition.

Abby let the boys figure out their own hierarchy, and she didn't feel it was her business to intervene unless someone was physically hurt. However, she did insist that her boys encourage each other. Ralph always had kind words for Fred's endeavors. But Fred seemed only to see where others were at fault or lacking. She worked closely with her eldest boy to instill more positive expressions of his thoughts, and she was delighted when she overheard Fred overcome his selfishness. "Ralphie, your drawings are very detailed and accurate. Maybe you'll be a famous artist someday," and then Fred gave his little brother a pat on the back.

This behavior was a vast improvement over what she'd witnessed one afternoon when the boys ran from the barn after finishing chores. Purposely, Fred tripped Ralph and then pushed him into a mud puddle. But this didn't seem to upset the younger boy. Instead of tears, Ralph took a handful of mud and squished it down on his brother's head, and then both boys laughed. When the boys marched into the mudroom, filthy and still laughing, Abby did not comment, just told them to get cleaned up immediately for dinner. It was a relief to see smaller Ralph stick up for himself.

Abijah insisted his sons treated each other with respect and affection. As a boy who spoke with a stammer, he knew first-hand how cruel people could be, and he wouldn't tolerate this in his children. He also had stern words if the boys didn't treat his animals kindly.

"What do you think Pa did to make Mother so angry, Fred?" asked Ralph. The two boys, Fred, ten, and Ralph, eight, walked together, up early to move the cows fresh from milking to the field behind the barns.

"Mother's always angry, Ralph. And stern and unbending. I believe it is because she's Quaker," replied Fred. The younger brother thought hard about this. He didn't believe his older brother was right. Something was very wrong with their parents. *There was very little laughter in the house. Had it always been this way?* Ralph tried to remember. Their mother and pa were serious, but they liked to play chess and read by the fire. Now everything was subdued, and Ralph noticed they didn't speak to each other unless it was about family or the ranch.

Fred had questions of his own. "Ralph, why do you think Pa loves his cows so much? I don't love them at all. I can't wait until I'm grown and can get away from this place." Fred said these things to highlight everything he hated about being the son of a dairyman.

"I like our ranch just fine, and besides, we have to help Pa. He needs us, Fred." Ralph climbed up on the fence and sat waiting for his big brother to finish closing the gate so the cows wouldn't go where they shouldn't.

Fred was solidly built with dark hair and piercing, blue eyes, while Ralph was thin and wiry, with auburn hair and pale gray eyes. Ralph had heard his parents describe their sons as quick-witted with fine minds and he thought that was a fair assessment. Of his brother, the younger boy knew he always had to let Fred win and think he was in charge if only to keep the peace between them. Fred was Mother's favorite and there was nothing that could be done to sway her—it was a sad fact of life. *Someday, we will know the truth of who is a better student with keener thoughts.*

"Of course, now we have to listen to Pa and help him, but Mother says we will go to college someday, and then we will never have to milk a cow ever again. Just smell that cow shit and sheep shit and chicken shit. It's everywhere," said Fred with disgust.

"Stop saying shit, Fred, it's not nice. Mother would be angry to hear you talk that way." Ralph frowned at his brother and jumped down from the fence.

"You're a baby," the older boy sneered. Then he punched Ralph hard on the arm with the knuckle of his middle finger raised for extra pain. Not quite satisfied, he shoved Ralph trying to knock him down into a cow patty as he walked away.

Ralph kept from falling and didn't make a sound but rubbed at the spot where Fred had hurt him. It would leave a bruise, just like all the other times. *Keep it up, Brother.*

He figured Fred was probably right about college, but Ralph was sensitive to his Pa's feelings. And he did like most of his chores, even if Fred didn't. The best part was all the thinking he could do when he worked with the animals. He supposed there were worse things to smell than cows.

As the time grew closer that Fred would graduate from high school, Abby was more and more focused on making the dream of Harvard Law School a reality for her son. Fred's grades were well above average, and she thought he had what it would take to survive at the prestigious school. After all, Abby's brother, Bradley, was an alumnus who had gone on to serve as the district attorney of Marin County in 1864 at age 26. Surely their sons would have careers just as brilliant as Brad's.

As a boy, Abijah had known little formal education, and he was determined to see his sons better off than he was. It was the right thing to send the boys back East to college, but it would be so hard for him to say goodbye to them.

"I suppose we will visit them in Cambridge, and they shall come home for the holidays."

"Perhaps we'll visit. I do think they'll be too busy with their studies to come though."

"They'll be so far away. We will miss them terribly."

"They will be fine at Harvard." Her mind was set. The East was where Fred and Ralph would go. Certainly not at Stanford, not for her children.

Fred graduated from high school with very high marks, but his grades were not quite enough to get him enrolled at Harvard for his undergraduate work. He would begin his studies at Santa Rosa Methodist College until he could transfer. Abby was furious and

Fred was bitterly disappointed and embarrassed. He spent weeks moping about the house.

Luckily for everyone, the two years that Fred was at college in Santa Rosa went by swiftly. The shame of late entry into Harvard forgotten, Fred was very excited to begin his junior year at the college of his original choice the next fall. Abijah had suggested a going away party to celebrate Fred's accomplishments and Ralph's graduation from high school. The boys were excited that their parents had agreed to have such a celebration in their honor. They'd use the grand ballroom Abijah had insisted upon when they built the farmhouse. Family and friends from the area had been invited and there would be food and drinks, music and dancing.

As the day of the party grew closer, Abijah and Abby worked hard to get everything accomplished on top of all of their regular chores.

"Do we have enough seating?" she asked.

"Not enough, the boys can help me make a few more benches. I thought we'd set them up along the edges of the ballroom. Is that what you had in mind?"

"Yes, that'll work. We haven't had a party up there in years. What did we used to do for seating?" Abby checked her list and marked items off as she went through it.

"I can't remember. I think we were too busy dancing to worry about sitting down."

"Don't leave those details to the last minute."

"I'll get started on Sunday. The benches will be rough, nothing fancy, but I'll have Fred and Ralph help me sand them good. We don't want our guests going home with splinters in their hind quarters."

"Splinters!! Ha!" Abby gave a belly laugh unlike anything Abijah had heard in a long time from her.

The boys went to San Francisco to be fitted for new suits, and Abijah decided he'd have a new one as well.

"Let me buy you a new dress, Abby," said Abijah.

"No, no need for that. My good black dress will serve," she replied. Abijah shook his head because he knew once his wife's mind was made up, that was all there was to it.

On the day before the party, Abby went straight up to the ballroom after breakfast. She carried a bucket and scrub brush.

"What are you doing, Wife?" Abijah called after her.

"A good cleaning is what's needed up there. I'll not have a dirty floor for the party."

"That's a lot of work. Can I help you?" He expected her to decline his offer.

"Yes, you can. Go out on the back porch and get another scrub brush and another bucket while you're at it."

Abijah was very surprised she'd accepted, but he was glad to help.

"And go to the kitchen and get some clean rags, too," she ordered.

Abby was already on her knees in one corner scrubbing furiously with hot lye and sand. Abijah took her bucket and poured out half into his bucket. He worked in the opposite corner with the foul concoction. He got down on his knees and began to scrub when he felt her watching him. He looked over his shoulder for a moment.

"Put your back into it, man. Scrub for all your worth," Abby chuckled.

They worked past supper time.

Abby stood up, wiping her brow. "We've missed our meal, but let's finish here first."

"I'm hungry, but you're in charge, Ma'am."

The last step was to wipe down the floor with clean rags and the job was done.

"Let's take all of this downstairs, and I'll fix us something to eat." After Abby finished putting together some leftovers, they sat quietly in the kitchen, eating steadily. Their hard work had yielded a companionable silence.

Fred and Ralph arrived home from last minute errands in Petaluma.

"Is there anything left to eat?" asked Ralph.

"Help yourself. There's plenty on the stove. Your father and I just spent most of the day cleaning upstairs so I'm not going to wait on you." Abby looked content after a long day's work.

"Everything's ready for tomorrow, boys. Nothing to do but wait for our guests' arrival," said Abijah.

"Would you care for a game of chess?" Abby asked her husband. Fred and Ralph looked at one another in surprise then sat down and ate leftover chicken and dumplings.

"That sounds fine." Abijah followed her into the parlor but said over his shoulder. "You boys clean up the kitchen for your mother, if you please."

The Secret Lives of Ancestors

The party was the most exciting thing to happen in Tomales in a long time. Relatives and friends came from San Francisco, Petaluma, Sebastopol, and Santa Rosa. Everyone came dressed in their best.

Abijah watched, pleased, as his younger son danced with one young lady and then another. *I wonder were Fred got to,* he thought. He scanned the dance floor until he saw his elder son in the corner; he was surrounded by several friends who listened intently as he held forth. Abijah couldn't tell what was being said but he could tell Fred was sermonizing passionately, red faced, blustery. The young people nodded in agreement every few seconds as he went on.

"What do you think he's going on about?" Abby joined her husband and watched the party with him.

"With Fred, you never know. But he looks quite pleased. Ralphie's enjoying himself, too."

"Yes." Then something caught his wife's eye and she moved across the dance floor to speak with her brother, Ike. *Too bad, Ike had never forgiven him*, Abijah mused. Abby hadn't either but at least they could be in the same room without trouble.

The party continued until ten that evening. The food and drink was splendid, and Abijah and Abby received many compliments and their sons were pleased.

After the last guest had gone and Ralph had thanked his parents for the party and his gifts, he'd gone to bed for the night. They'd given Ralph his gifts earlier, a book by Wordsworth from Mother, and a set oil paints and brushes from Father.

Fred and his parents stayed up talking in the parlor about events of the evening. "Here, Fred, I have this for you. I think it will come in very handy when you are at school next year," said Mother.

He removed the plain wrapping paper from a blue leather-covered book. It was a small volume, entitled *The Correct Thing in Good Society,* and his mother had engraved his name on the cover. It was a book on etiquette for any situation a young person might find themselves in. Fred flipped through the pages and thought the book would be very useful in his adult life.

"Thank you, Mother, for the thoughtful gift. And thank you for the wonderful party. Ralph and I enjoyed ourselves immensely."

"You are welcome," she said. Fred noticed she seemed tired tonight. His parents were getting on in years and this late night had taken its toll on them.

"I have something for you too, Fred. I thought this might be an appropriate gift." Father handed him a small package tied with string. Fred opened it—a gold pocket watch.

"Thank you, Father. It is very fine." Fred attached the chain to the button on his vest and held the watch out to see if it kept good time. He looked at the mantle clock; yes, the time was just right. Before he snapped it shut, he read the inscription. *To Fred from your father, Tempus Fugit, Memento Mori.* He snapped it shut with a disconcerted expression on his face and put the watch into his trouser pocket. What a strange sentiment. His father could be rather odd. Honestly, he'd expected a monetary gift from his parents, but how could he ask them for more after they'd given him such a lovely party. He wished they'd consulted him. He would have told them exactly what he wanted—an investment in his future.

"I know the inscription is serious, Fred, but this is the beginning of your life, and you have much to accomplish. 'Time flies, remember death.' Just a bit of advice from your dear old pa." Father winked, trying to lighten the mood, but it was too late.

Fred was curt when he said his goodnights feeling vaguely irritated with everything and everyone. His parents didn't even realize anything had upset him.

A few months before Ralph graduated from high school he'd had a serious talk with his parents. "Although Harvard's ready for me in the fall, I'd like to defer for a year."

"You'll do no such thing," his mother cried.

Abijah said nothing, choosing to wait to hear what his son had to say.

"Mother, I have to. For several reasons. Fred deserves to begin Harvard on his own. It was a terrible blow to his ego to have to begin his college years at Santa Rosa and you both know it." His parents nodded in agreement. "He didn't say much about it to you, but he was very candid with me. He needs to forge his own path in Massachusetts without the benefit of his younger brother weighing him down."

"I would agree with you, Ralph," said Abijah. "But you said there were other reasons."

"Yes. I submitted some of my writing to local papers and they've expressed interest. I'm going to try my hand at the newspaper game and hopefully sell some articles. It will be a valuable experience before I settle back down at school. And you both know how competitive Fred is. If he feels I'm going beyond what he's capable of, he can be very unpleasant and I should like to have a good relationship with my brother, if possible."

"I don't like it when he bullies you, Ralph. He cannot always get his own way." Abijah was annoyed by Fred's neediness, but it wouldn't do for Ralph to see him this way so he tried to keep himself under control.

Abby approved of Ralph's reasoning. "It sounds to me as though you've thought it through. I think a year's deferral is a good plan."

Abijah was still miffed not only with Fred, but with his wife too. He didn't understand why she couldn't see through Fred's manipulations.

Abby and Abijah were in the middle of one of their evening games of chess when Fred and Ralph rushed into the parlor. The boys were celebrating their last few months before Fred began at Harvard and had come up with a plan for their summer. They wanted to speak with their parents but knew better than to interrupt the game. So they sat in front of the fire and watched as their parents moved the chess pieces over the board. Abijah seemed to be winning, but Abby was concentrating fiercely.

"Checkmate." She had such a look of triumph on her face.

"Didn't see that coming." Abijah shook his head with feigned disappointment.

"That was quite a game, Mother," said Ralph.

"We have decided how we shall spend this summer," Fred announced, although his tone belied his excitement.

"What are your plans?" asked their father.

"We'd like to visit Aunt Mary and Uncle Amasa in Sisson. We plan to hunt and fish and we hope to climb Mount Shasta."

"Fred, don't you think it would be better to spend your summer preparing for school?" asked his mother.

"Mother," Fred looked down his nose. "I'm as prepared as I'm going to get."

"Let the boys go, Abby. It will do them good," said Abijah.

"I suppose you're right," she conceded.

"We better send word to my sister right away," said Abijah. "I'd heard they've had some financial worries. I would not add difficulties to their lives, and we must not make them feel obligated beyond their means. Perhaps I can suggest that you boys could work part of the summer to pay for your room and keep?"

"As long as it doesn't interfere with my plans," said Fred. He didn't want to work even one minute.

"I don't mind, Pa. No reason we couldn't help our aunt and uncle." Fred scowled at his younger brother. He'd tell Ralph later exactly what he thought about helping out.

Abijah received a letter from Mary the following week. She wrote that Fred and Ralph could stay as long as they wished, and

Amasa agreed to let the boys work for him at the mill to cover their expenses.

Ralph and Fred made plans to leave in the latter part of June. Family friends, Mrs. William Van Arsdale and her daughter Katie, were returning to their home in Sisson for the summer, and would accompany the boys on their trip. Katie was keen to climb Mount Shasta with the brothers, and Ralph had romantic ideas about Katie. He had hopes that by summer's end she might return those feelings.

Chapter Fourteen
Mount Shasta and Beyond

In June of 1888, Fred and Ralph took the train into Sacramento and, from there, north to Sisson. They'd fully discussed the idea of traveling by stagecoach, as it would have been a much less expensive trip. At the last minute, their parents surprised them by paying for their train fare and the boys were grateful not to have to spend so much time on a bumpy ride.

Once they began the northern climb beyond the town of Redding, everyone on the train marveled at the change in scenery. The steep cliffs and dense forest rolled by as each mile brought them closer to Mount Shasta. Even in summer, the beautiful giant still had patches of snow near its summit. Today, the highest peaks, which were usually enshrouded in strange cloud formations, were visible in the clear blue sky.

"Do you think we'll make it to the top? Maybe it's beyond our ability," said Fred.

Of course, he was apprehensive but Ralph refused to let him ruin his adventure.

"I have to summit. I promised a story to the newspaper."

Fred was already thinking of other things. "Look, that's where I want to go." He pointed to the rock outcropping of Castle Crags. "I've studied the area some, beyond that ridge should be Castle Lake. Plenty of good fishing, and a good spot to camp."

Ralph nodded in agreement. "It would be nice to go up to the lake for the day even if we don't have time to stay overnight." He stared out of the windows on the opposite side of the train as it rolled along. He didn't say any more about Shasta. There was nothing to be gained by arguing about it now.

"You boys will want to see this! Come sit on this side of the train," Mrs. Van Arsdale exclaimed.

"We're coming upon Mossbrae Falls," added Katie.

On the right side, they were treated to a view of the most beautiful waterfalls nearly obscured by lush forest. The water poured off moss and fern-covered cliffs into the pools created by the Sacramento River, the bank closest to the onlookers was covered in smooth rock. There was a small beach—how refreshing a swim in the clear water would feel. It looked like a perfect retreat on a hot day.

The brothers arrived at the train station in Sisson weary from the trip. "Fred, there they are." Ralph waved at his aunt and uncle who were waiting for them in their farm wagon. They collected their bags and rushed over to meet them.

"It's good to see you boys." Amasa helped them load in their cases. "Let's go. Mary's supper is waiting back home."

"How was the train?" Mary asked.

"Very much preferable to the coach and so much faster. Our parents bought the tickets," Fred boasted.

"Well, you're here now and I'm glad of it. Settle in and enjoy the views on the way home."

Ralph stared in awe as Shasta rose before them. "Gives me shivers."

As soon as they arrived at the house, Aunt Mary got supper on the table. Everyone tucked in and conversation was sparse as they filled up on her cooking.

Fred set down his fork and wiped his mouth with a napkin. "Thank you for your hospitality." He was finally relaxed and in much better humor.

Aunt Mary got up from the table and began stacking plates, "We're delighted to have you, boys."

"The meal was delicious," Ralph commented.

"Hope you saved room for blackberry cobbler." Mary brought in plates heaped with the treat. "And I want to hear all about Abijah and your mother."

"They are well," Fred reported drily. "Busy with Pa's cows, as ever."

"I wish they could come visit sometime. I miss my brother's wit something fierce," Mary said.

"I know he misses you too, Aunt. I've got letters from them both." Ralph dug into his coat pocket and retrieved a small packet from his parents.

Aunt Mary looked pleased. "I'll just read these later."

"Uncle Amasa, what will you have us do to earn our keep?" Ralph asked.

At the mention of work, Fred kicked him hard on the shin and Ralph let out a startled grunt. He reached down to rub his ankle, and shot his brother a dirty look. If her expression was any indication, Aunt Mary had noticed the exchange.

"Everything alright, Ralph?" she asked, eyes narrowed.

"A bit sore from the jostling of the train, Aunt," he fibbed.

Amasa let out a short braying laugh that surprised both boys. "I sure can use your help. We're busy at the lumber mill and can also use additional crew."

"Husband, you won't have them doing anything dangerous, will you?"

"Oh, of course not. These boys are here on holiday. But I have a few projects, they can help out with."

"And, we're happy to work for you," said Fred. Ralph snickered. Working was the last thing his brother wanted to do.

"I've also been hired by the *Argus* to write a few stories about this area. Once we've completed our trek up the mountain, I hope to sell the story to more than just the *Argus*."

"You'd best check with *The Sisson Mascot*, Ralph. Maybe you can sell a few lines to them as well. The owner's a friend of mine, Mr. R. Beers Loos. Later this week, you can come with me to his office, and I'll make introductions," Amasa winked at his nephew.

"Thank you, that's wonderful. I'll bring a few of my stories. You never know, maybe he'll be interested." Ralph looked over at Fred to see if he had any comment about his plans, but he was being ignored.

Finally, Fred got to the heart of what he was interested in. "Uncle, what can you tell me about the hunting? I've heard there are bears up here."

"Oh, there's plenty and you can sell the hides. You can even sell the meat for a few dollars. There's deer hunting up here, too," he said. "And, I've been threatening to go down the hill to the McCloud River for fishing; maybe you boys would like to come along."

"We'd be very pleased to join you," said Ralph.

Later, when they were getting ready to sleep for the night, he scolded Fred.

"We are obligated to help our family, Fred. I know you have lots of plans, but the work comes first. We cannot expect our aunt and uncle to feed us and shelter us all summer for free." Ralph kept thinking about his pa and how he'd want the boys to treat his sister and her husband.

"Oh, you sound just like Mother and I'm sick of it. I'm willing to work, and you know it. I just had hopes of a few free days before getting back to the grindstone. But the way *you've* set it up, we'll be working at first light."

"If that's the case, then we better go to sleep, Brother." In Ralph's estimation, Fred was spoiled and never considered others first.

They laid quietly in their beds for a time and then Ralph asked his brother about Katie. He knew it was probably a mistake since Fred was still sore with him. "Do you think Katie Van Arsdale would be a good match?"

"Are you joking? You're too young, so don't even bother thinking about her. No. Not a good match." Yes, Fred was definitely still mad.

"No, Brother. I don't think I'm too young," he insisted.

"Her family is quite influential in these parts, and I don't think she'd be interested in a boy like you. Not really. She's more likely to think of you as a brother instead of husband material, I'd say." Fred wore a smug expression.

He could really be cruel when he had a mind to, Ralph thought. "Katie's only a year older than me. I danced with her twice at the party, and I thought we were getting along splendidly. It seemed as though she liked me." As the words came out, Ralph thought about it and realized Fred was probably right, and it stung.

"It's obvious she's just being polite." Fred ended the conversation by turning over to sleep and within a few minutes he was snoring.

At breakfast the following day, their uncle quieted any qualms Fred had about working too soon.

"I want to show you boys around the lumber mill today. Then I'll take you out for a grand meal and give a tour around town. Does that sound like a good first day in Sisson?"

"Amasa, you're taking them to the El Monte? If my sister-in-law finds out you've taken her sons to a saloon, she'll probably never speak to me again." Aunt Mary looked partly worried but mostly amused.

"Mary, I'm only taking them for lunch at the hotel. It's a perfectly respectable establishment."

"Don't worry about our mother. We won't tell her about the saloon part. Obviously, there's no need for that," Fred quickly reassured his aunt and uncle.

As soon as Amasa, Fred, and Ralph left the house, Mary sat down to begin a letter to her favorite brother. She thought about his children, how different they were from him. *Must be Abby's influence.* Fred seemed moody and pretentious—Mary didn't think she could tolerate being in his presence if it hadn't been for the calming influence of his brother. Where the older boy was a braggart, Ralph seemed quite humble. And it was clear that of the two, he was the more intelligent. The thing that bothered her most was that Abijah's dream of his children taking over the dDairy would never happen. He'd created a very lucrative business and now that his sons were to be attorneys, as soon as he was too old to work, the business would dissolve. Of course, every parent wanted success for their children, and wanted the younger generation to have more. But still, Mary was sad for Abijah. It must be bittersweet for him.

Hours later, Mary heard them laughing and carrying on as they tromped up the front steps. It didn't take long before she realized that Amasa must have ordered several rounds of drinks at the saloon. *Were they drunk?* Mary rolled her eyes, exasperated. Her husband had done exactly the opposite as what he said he would, and Abby Woodworth could never find out about this day.

She opened the front door to usher them into the house.

"Get yourselves cleaned up, dinner in a few minutes." Mary disappeared into the kitchen to finished getting their meal prepared. She tried not to be angry with Amasa, but it was a test of her patience.

As it turned out, Fred had nothing to fear about having enough free time in his schedule. The boys worked at the lumber mill four mornings a week and had afternoons and evenings free, as well as three full days of liberty. There was plenty of time for them to explore, fish, and hunt.

Abijah's sons were hard workers, and Amasa had no regrets about having them work at the mill. He paid them the same wages each week that any new man at the mill would receive, and the money would help finance Fred and Ralph's climb up Mount Shasta.

Fred was hunting for the weekend, and in his absence, Ralph was invited for lunch by Mary and Amasa's daughter, his first cousin, Cora Bowles. Cora and Katie Van Arsdale were best friends, so Katie had been invited to join them for lunch, too.

"Katie, will you join me on a hike to Castle Lake tomorrow? I want a good view of Shasta, and it is supposed to be a beautiful area," said Ralph.

Katie didn't answer Ralph immediately. Instead, she sipped her coffee and looked out the window as she searched for the right words.

Cora saved Katie the trouble by answering. "If Katie goes, Ralph, I think I should go along, too. What do you think, Jesse?" she asked her husband.

"I'd go, but I've got a shipment to unload at the mercantile."

"That's too bad, I wish you could come. Katie, you don't want to miss it. The views are spectacular," said Cora.

"How can I say no to that?" said Katie. She was relieved her friend would come on the hike. Katie knew Ralph wanted to court her and she had no interest in a romantic relationship, so she was careful not to encourage him. She certainly didn't want to hurt his feelings. They both had a love of all things in nature, but that wasn't enough for her to consider marriage. If Cora came along, Ralph wouldn't have any opportunity to say something they'd both regret. "It's too bad Fred's not able to join us," she added.

"He won't be back until tomorrow evening. Fred's determined to shoot a bear. He talked about it our whole trip from home and hasn't stopped yet."

Ralph, Katie, and Cora left early the next morning and rode the ten miles to Castle Lake by pack horses they'd rented in town. The horses were sturdy and just right for trails.

Not far from where they hoped to picnic, they saw an enormous black bear. It looked in their direction, bellowed once, and then wandered away to a distant spot on the far side of the little lake. They watched in fascination as it waded into the water and began 'fishing'.

They weren't in immediate danger, but the three kept their eyes on the beast as they ate the picnic lunch Cora had brought. Once they realized the bear had no interest in them, they were able to relax. They sat on rocks near the water's edge and took in the magic of the place. Mountain breezes blew the scents of pine and cedar from up high, pleasant and acrid. The sun glinted off the lake, and they watched as fish jumped and created sprays of water that caught the light. They spied a bald eagle as it caught drafts and glided through the air, circling for prey. They heard the insistent taps of woodpeckers searching for their supper.

"I think I'll ask Fred if he'd like to come back up here with me for a few days of camping. I'll bet that lake is full of fish," said Ralph.

Too soon, it was time for the journey back to Sisson. Ralph got the horses ready while Cora and Katie packed up their belongings. It was a three-hour ride in each direction and a lot of trouble for only one day, but all agreed that the scenery was magnificent.

"Jesse, I'm so sorry you couldn't come with us. The views were stunning," exclaimed Cora.

"We brought along a field glass and were able to see to the town of Sisson with Shasta rising above all, and Mount Hood," said Ralph.

"I'm sorry I missed out, but I'm glad you're back home safe," Jesse said.

"I wished I'd had Fred's rifle along. We came upon a huge black bear. It was ahead of us as we made our way to the lake. Luckily as soon as the bear spotted us, he moved away. Trout was much more interesting than we were."

The moment Ralph mentioned the bear, he knew he shouldn't have. Jesse frowned. "You really shouldn't be out in the wilderness without a firearm, Ralph. If I'd have known, I'd have sent you with mine."

"Well, we were safe," said Cora with a hint of exasperation. She shot a look at Ralph and he was uncomfortable knowing he'd vexed his cousin.

"Next time, we'll bring the rifle," Ralph said, trying to make amends.

"Jesse, it was a thoroughly beautiful day," said Katie. "The lake was clean and clear, and it was a lovely way to spend the day. After viewing Shasta from that vantage point, I'm more excited to hike it than ever!"

When Fred returned from his hunting trip, he had, indeed, shot a black bear at a distance of thirty feet. One shot went in over the left eye and came out the right shoulder. He sold the bear meat and had the hide processed to bring back home to his parents.

"Ed Stewart will be leading our party up the mountain," said Katie. "I'm disappointed but Mr. Chamberlain was injured his last trip up the mountain and isn't quite ready yet to make another trip. Everyone else in the party wants to go tomorrow, Ralph. What do you want to do?"

"I want to wait for Chamberlain, of course. He's best qualified for the trip. Who is this Ed Stewart? Has he summitted Shasta?"

"No, but he tried. Last year was his first year up, but he didn't make it. Weather didn't permit."

"So we're to go with a guide that's never actually made it to the top. That's bad form, Katie, and I don't feel good about this."

"He's Cora and Jesse's friend, and I feel uncomfortable saying no. I wouldn't want to hurt their feelings."

"I suppose we must go along then and make the best of it," replied Ralph.

The next day, at one-thirty in the afternoon, the nine-person party left Sisson to ascend Mount Shasta. Fred returned just in time to join Ralph, Katie, Mrs. Van Arsdale, Cora, Mr. Stewart, and three other men. The first part of the journey was on horseback, and after traveling twelve miles, they'd reached the immediate base of Shasta. They camped overnight in a miserable little shelter; it was a frigid and uneasy night but sleep finally came.

"Fred. Fred, wake up. We've overslept. It's after four in the morning. Shouldn't we already be hiking?" Ralph was worried and with good cause.

Ed Stewart heard the comment and replied. "Don't worry. We'll have plenty of time to summit. Last year, when I made my attempt, I left about this time."

"Did you consider this was why you didn't make it? Everything I've read states that climbers should leave lower camp no later than two-thirty in the morning," Ralph argued until he saw Cousin Cora frowning at him. The guide shrugged and walked away from the conversation.

There were a few more grumbling remarks, but everyone was packed up and ready to go by five-thirty. They'd smeared burnt cork on their faces to protect from the harmful rays of the sun.

"You all look simply ghastly," Fred remarked sourly.

"Here, Brother, put some of this on your face. You'll burn otherwise." Ralph tried to get it on his brother's nose, but Fred pushed him away.

"Ralph, I'm not wearing that ridiculous stuff. I know what I'm doing and I'll be fine."

"Alright, Fred. Where are your protective glasses? Didn't you buy any?"

"It's a waste of money. My hat will be plenty of protection. You know I'm not one for spending money haphazardly. And I don't have hobnails for my boots, so don't bother asking." Ralph just shook his head in frustration; this was typical Fred behavior. He worried that his brother would hurt himself just to save a dollar, but there was no point arguing with him. Fred was a little too much like their mother when it came to matters of spending.

The ladies were dressed in bloomers and wore thick woolen stockings underneath with men's heavy socks on top. They laughed about their attire. Everyone wore many layers of woolen sweaters piled up and leather gloves under woolen mittens. They carried Alpine Stocks to aid them later in their climb.

Ralph tried to imagine what his mother might think of the ladies in his group. He wasn't sure if she'd be pleased to see young women who were brave and just as capable as the men in the group, or would she think them unseemly?

The group traveled by horse for two more miles, then left them to graze contentedly while they continued on foot. The sun began to rise as the party reached the snowline.

Immediately, their guide seemed confused about which trail they should use in their ascent up the mountain. His excuse was that there wasn't as much snow at this elevation last year when he made his attempt. Finally, he settled hastily on a route to quell the grumbling of his party. As they began their climb, everyone focused on their footing and tried to ignore Mr. Stewart's ineptness.

The heat from the sun beat down upon the southwestern slope of the mountain, and chunks of ice and rock loosened by the warmth began to cascade down the hill toward the climbers. All were wary of being hit by shards; caution was of utmost importance, and Mr. Stewart's group continued the upward climb.

Fred watched in surprise as the flying debris came hurtling towards him and hollered, "Avalanche! I'm hit! I'm hit!" Down he went to his knees in the snow. Ralph turned back to his brother to assess the injury.

"Is he alright?" shouted Katie, breathless.

"You keep climbing. I'll see to him," Ralph replied.

He bent over his brother but couldn't see where Fred had been hit.

"My back, Ralph, it hurts." He helped him get up and Fred's eyes widened with surprise and he scrambled away just as more rocks came towards them. He issued no warning and left Ralph in the pathway of the bullet-like chunks. Unaware of the immediate danger, Ralph didn't move fast enough out of the way and was struck on his left temple.

"Ouch!" yelped Ralph. Stunned by his injury, he rubbed at the site, and his hand came away bloody. Refusing to let it stop him, he called out, "Come on, Fred, keep going. Let's catch up with the group." His head stung, and he felt a ringing in his ears, but Ralph was determined to push onward.

The air was thin, and it became more challenging for the climbers to breathe as they struggled upward. The sun reflected dangerously and they suffered an unquenchable thirst. Fred's face became more burnt with each passing minute, and he was limping. The wound on Ralph's head continued oozing blood and throbbed painfully with each beat of his heart, but he remained silent and focused. The more Fred complained about his 'wounds,' the more Ralph determined to remain staunch and didn't offer complaint.

The injuries sustained by the falling rocks frightened the inexperienced guide. He realized too late it was beyond his ability to lead his party further. One of the ladies noticed clouds gathering quickly in the near distance and informed the others. Their already uneasy group accepted that the weather had taken a turn. The dangers of the trail gathered momentum the higher they climbed.

Almost too late, Mr. Stewart halted the climbers and announced, "We have injured persons in our party. I believe it would be prudent for us to give up ascent. Sadly, we shall not summit today—conditions are not right." There were sounds of disappointment amongst the group, but all were in agreement. They must turn back.

The descent was even more dangerous than the trek up the face. The climbers were exhausted, stretched nearly beyond their limits. The ice made footing slippery, particularly for Fred who had not prepared properly. He steadied himself by holding his walking sticks in one hand and clutching Ralph's shoulder with the other.

Finally, they reached a smooth enough patch of ice where they could sit down upon the burlap sacks they'd packed. With the protection from the ice under their rear-ends, they slid with frightening speed more than a mile down the steep mountain. They used the drag of the Alpine Stocks behind them as a sort of braking mechanism to aid in slowing their rate of travel. All the while, their screams were swallowed by the mountain as they gathered speed in their descent. Each member prayed for safe deliverance to the bottom. Finally, they slid to a stop and hiked safely the rest of the way down to where they'd left their horses to graze. They arrived exhilarated and thankful to have made it back alive.

The Secret Lives of Ancestors

As soon as Ralph had his wounds attended by the town doctor and rested up a few days, he made plans to retry the summit. Unfortunately, Cora was unable to go. Fred refused to go up that "damned" mountain under any circumstances, but Katie agreed to try again, and they went with their first choice of guides, Mr. Chamberlain, who had recovered from his injuries.

Three days later, Ralph Woodworth successfully summitted Mount Shasta. At the top, he and Katie spent half an hour taking in the view of two hundred miles in all directions. It was a beautifully clear day and worth the effort, worth the danger. Everyone in the party signed the logbook and added their names to the monument at the top.

"Fred, I painted my name, Ralph Woodworth '88, next to a 'Joe Kirk '87.' Katie painted her name underneath. It was truly breathtaking and we made the descent safely in two hours," Ralph excitedly reported to his brother that night as they readied themselves for sleep.

"It should have been my name up there with yours, Ralph. I did *practically* summit. It wasn't my fault things went wrong, you know. You are lucky you made it alive, Brother," Fred said, shaking his head in disappointment.

"I'm sorry you didn't come along, but you were quite adamant about not risking your life. Are you having regrets now, Fred?" asked Ralph. Surely he didn't expect his brother to write his name in the book or paint his name on the monument, did he?

"Have you told our parents about your injury?" Fred asked sullenly.

"No, why don't you tell them? You are good at relating all the details. I'm turning in for the night."

The rest of the summer flew by. The young men enjoyed many pleasant hours fishing and hunting, and hiking near the town of Sisson. After summiting Mount Shasta, Ralph stopped pursuing Katie Van Arsdale. He still liked her, but it was obvious she didn't return his feelings. Instead, he focused on his writing and submitted his accounts of both treks up the mountain to several newspapers.

His stories were wildly popular and Ralph became a minor celebrity about town. Alone in their room one night, Fred griped about the attention his little brother had garnered. "I really don't know why; it's not like you shot a bear or lead the climb," he said in annoyance.

Ralph rolled his eyes. "No need to be petty, Brother."

"Thank you, Aunt Mary, Uncle Amasa. I enjoyed every minute of my stay with you. I hope we weren't too much trouble," said Ralph as he shook his uncle's hand and kissed his aunt on the cheek.

"Oh, you boys were no trouble at all. I hope you had a pleasant time too, Fred? I'm sorry you didn't get more bears. I know your heart was set on the hunting," said Aunt Mary.

"Yes, Aunt, it was quite pleasant. Thank you for having us. Thank you, Uncle," Fred replied very formally with a little bow.

Fred and Ralph boarded the train, alone this time with only their aunt and uncle on hand to see them off. Fred took his seat immediately by the window and turned as far away from his brother as he could. Ralph shrugged, amused by his brother's attempt to insult and took out his journal to make some notes. He was anxious to get home and tell his parents about his adventures.

A few weeks after the young men returned home from Sisson, it was time to bid Fred farewell before he left for Cambridge. The brothers were parting on a sour note. During their last days together, they hadn't gotten along well with minor disagreements getting blown out of all proportion, and the boys squabbled over the most trivial things. Ralph realized that instead of strengthening their bonds, they had grown further apart than they were before. He was sad about the fracture between the two of them but couldn't see how it was to be repaired. Strangely, Fred didn't seem to notice or care that anything was amiss.

"Goodbye, Fred. I hope you enjoy your time at Harvard," said Ralph. Their parents waited out in the wagon to take Fred to the train station, and he wanted to wish his brother well.

"Yes, I will enjoy Harvard. We'll be together next year. Don't miss me too much, Brother."

In fact, Ralph did not miss his older brother at all. The last few years with him had been tiresome and he was finished making excuses for Fred's bad behavior. He'd been making concessions since they were boys and he'd had enough.

Without Fred as a distraction, Ralph applied himself even more rigorously to his writing. Abby and Abijah couldn't help but notice how much their younger son seemed to flourish without the influence of his older brother. Ralph was quicker, more physically fit, more sensitive, and although a carefully guarded secret, Ralph was more intelligent.

When he wasn't writing, Ralph had taken ownership of his mother's violin, and she didn't mind a bit, as it had been years since she'd played—it was too painful on her arthritis and Abijah didn't care for the sound. Ralph often went up to the gum tree forest to practice. The notes rose above on the breeze and lent a most haunting quality to the experience. He loved the sweet, melancholy sounds echoing through the trees. He found there was something sacred about the music of nature blending with the violin.

He even had time to paint, which he'd given up on last year. Suddenly, he was free to use not only his mind but his imagination, and he took full advantage of this burst of creativity. He painted several nature studies, including a boy fishing at dusk in an area that looked much like the headwaters of the Sacramento River. When he was finished with it, he had it framed and presented it to his parents.

When his year off completed, Ralph left for Cambridge without any fanfare. There were no parties, no grand gifts. And that was fine with Ralph. He had his sights set on a grand tour of Europe between college and university, and every penny he saved went towards that dream. He hadn't shared his plan with anyone yet, but he knew his parents wouldn't deny him the opportunity. He just needed to make sure that Fred was not allowed to invite himself along.

As Fred recommended, Ralph went to San Francisco and had two fine suits made before leaving for the East. Fred had mentioned that when he arrived at school, he'd been without the proper attire expected of a law student, and it had been terribly embarrassing. He hoped to spare his younger brother the same awkwardness he'd had to endure.

Ralph thrived in his undergraduate years and enjoyed everything about being a student at Harvard. Fred had his own comrades that he studied with and socialized with and made it clear that Ralph should find his own way and his own friends. At first, he was disappointed with his brother, but as time went on, he realized that it was better for him to keep his studies and social life separate from Fred.

Sometimes there were whole weeks when he and Fred didn't speak, and he found that he didn't mind it. Of course, he never made mention of this to his parents; they wouldn't understand. As far as they were concerned, Fred was taking wonderful care of his younger brother.

A classmate of Fred's approached Ralph one afternoon in the library. "You're Fred Woodworth's brother, Ralph."

"I am, but you have me at a disadvantage, Sir."

"My apologies, I'm in Fred's study group. Walter Andrews."

The two young men shook hands, and then there was an awkward pause. Walter seemed nervous, unclear how to proceed.

"Was there something in particular you needed? I'm on my way to class."

"Oh, sorry to hold you up. I was just wondering, that is to say, I'm curious about your brother." He flushed and stammered and tugged uncomfortably at his shirt collar as though he was being choked. "I mean, exactly, what type of law do you see Fred entering into?"

"Well, that's a mighty strange question. Why don't you ask him?" At this moment, Ralph found himself both vexed and intrigued.

"I have. We have asked him, and he hasn't seen fit to answer. Of course, he has time to decide, but we're curious. And it might affect us overall, to have an undecided man in our group." Walter looked slightly sick now. "Please don't say anything to Fred. We don't want to upset his plans. We just want to know."

"Huh. I don't know what his plans are. You may have noticed, he doesn't confide in me. Yes, we are working together on behalf of our uncle's estate, but I'm behind him in age and education, so he has me doing the research. Of course, our business is very private, so he won't want to discuss it with anyone outside of the family."

Ralph chose his next words carefully. "I have often wondered if Fred possesses the compassion and moral compass needed to be an excellent attorney. Certainly, he is dogged in his pursuit. He comes at a thing with a scientific mind, but is it enough, I wonder, for him to be a very great man of law?" Walter stared at Ralph in shock at the personal nature of his words.

That sealed it, Ralph thought. If this got back to his brother, he'd be in for it not only with Fred but with his mother, too. But he was tired of keeping silent; tired of being second best. He'd deal with the backlash, should it come. But maybe Fred's so-called friends wouldn't reveal his disloyalty. Maybe he wasn't alone in how he felt about his brother.

Chapter Fifteen
Rules of Engagement

Fred became keenly and surprisingly interested in football while at Harvard. He never would have imagined it, but he very much enjoyed attending the games. Harvard Crimson was to play against the Yale Bulldogs and he'd decided to go down to New Haven with several of his classmates.

At that same game, a group of young ladies from Vassar College were attending. Two of the girls had brothers who played on the Harvard team and they'd made the trip to cheer them on. They introduced themselves to the boys from Cambridge and were delighted when they were invited to sit with Fred's group.

It didn't take him long to notice the girl with the auburn hair. She was lovely and had a beautiful smile. She must have felt Fred staring, because she turned to him and smiled again, but then waited for him to start the conversation. It was all he could do to get a few words out.

"Hello. My name is Fred Woodworth." He leaned forward in a slight bow and held out his hand in greeting. She took his cold hand in her gloved hand—it was terribly chilly sitting in the stands.

"I'm Mildred Mathes. Pleased to meet you, Fred Woodworth."

She had a soft drawl and exquisite manners. Fred wondered if she came from a wealthy family. Surely she must, to be able to attend college so far from her home which he learned was in Memphis.

As the game continued, Fred continued his appraisal. Her clothing was of fine quality, nothing ostentatious, but definitely not cheap. She was bundled up in long woolen coat, woolen scarf, and leather gloves, but she wore a fetching navy colored hat that sported a little plume of dark feathers and he noticed at her neck a beautiful cameo brooch. Understated quality, he thought.

Her accent was utterly charming although he could only catch one in every five words, but that might have been due to the deafening sounds emanating from the crowds in the stands. He'd very much like to visit with her under more sedate circumstances. He wondered if she would consider it. Fred was smitten.

Mildred was very interested to get to know Fred Woodworth better. He was handsome. His hair was dark, nearly black and he wore a mustache and beard which she thought could use a bit of tidying up. His eyes were more silvery than blue—his gaze was penetrating, which would be perfect for a lawyer. He was in his last year of law school and appeared studious and thoughtful. She thought he must be of above average intelligence. He was a bit on the shy side, but also possessed an inner self-confidence when he expressed his ideas about the law and his future, and Mildred found the contradiction intriguing. She wondered if her papa would approve of him but was quite sure her mama would like him. There was the problem of him being a Yankee that would have to be overcome, but she didn't see it as too daunting. At least, she hoped not.

After their first chance meeting, they spent every bit of free time together in groups with friends in New York, Boston, or somewhere along the way. Fred fell in love quickly and professed his feelings. But Mildred was reserved and did not share what was in her mind right away. She was a pragmatic woman and more accustomed to the rules of courtship than Fred. She felt it was much too forward for a young lady to declare her fondness very soon. After all, there were proprieties to be observed, and Mildred was very proper.

It was the beginning of April before the two found themselves able to have an entire afternoon together. There was still a chill in the air leftover from winter, but the blossoms were beginning to appear on the fruit trees, and the sun was shining after a long, cold season. They picnicked in a park near the Vassar campus. Fred was in New York for some family business, so it was a perfect opportunity to meet with Mildred.

In addition to their visits back and forth, they'd been exchanging letters each week as well. Mildred wanted to learn more about California and, of course, Fred's family. She'd shared much of her childhood with him, but he had remained quiet about his.

"Tell me about your family, your parents. What was life like growing up at your house?" They had just finished lunch and were sitting very close to one another with their backs against an ancient oak tree.

"I am the eldest, and my brother, whom you have met, is two years younger. We always knew we'd go to Harvard. Mother talked about her sons being attorneys from the first time I could remember." There was no warmth in his voice; he was only reciting facts. "My father has a spread in Tomales, California, near the Pacific Ocean. One thousand acres of rolling hills, dairy cows, sheep, a couple of pigs, a few horses, chickens, dogs, and of course cats in the barns to keep the mice and rats under control."

"I don't know much about dairy farms or taking care of livestock. Tell me what it was like to grow up with all of those animals. It seems like it might be wonderful." Mildred and Fred were holding hands, and she leaned her head on his shoulder and listened to him speak.

"I can tell you, I know more about cows, chickens, sheep, and pigs than any person should have to know," Fred chuckled. "Ralph and I spent our time helping my father run the place. Of course, he had ranch hands, but Father did most of the work with Ralph and me. We could have used a lot of modern farm equipment to make the work easier, but Father wouldn't hear of it; he did things the old-fashioned way. We boys had our farm work every day, seven days a week from the time we could walk until we came east for school. That was on top of our regular chores and, of course, our studies. We would never think to complain because our father and mother worked harder than anyone else on the place, and to gripe would have been disrespectful.

"Everything on the property, including miles and miles of fencing was built by my father and mother in the early years of their marriage. I would be giving you the wrong idea were I to neglect to tell you how impressive The Tomales is."

"It sounds magnificent, Fred," Mildred interjected.

"The Tomales was Father's dream and by virtue of marriage, Mother's. But she had bigger plans for us boys. She was a mathematician and took a job as a schoolteacher when she came to live in California. Mother is brilliant, but being a woman, always felt that she could not do the things she dreamed of and so Ralph and I were made to fulfill her dreams."

Mildred knew well the inequities of being a woman in this world. Her father and brothers never told her she couldn't do as she liked, but she understood the rules of society. "Your mother and I have a lot in common, Fred. Someday, maybe things will be different for us, but for now, we must take the few opportunities we can."

Fred continued his observations after a few moments. "Father has his own kind of intelligence—he's an expert when it comes to his bossies, his dairy, and knows the land like the back of his hand. He calls the cows his ladies, which puts Mother in a proper fury." Fred smiled to think of his father and all those cows. "Before they married, they agreed that their children would be educated to be lawyers with no thought of being ranchers or farmers." Mildred wondered what this agreement had cost his father. It must have been hard for him to lose his sons to Harvard.

"What was your best memory of your parents, Fred?"

"When we were children, Ralph and I loved to watch our parents play chess in the evenings. I know that sounds dull, but they were so good at it. It was almost like watching them dance or sometimes like watching a battle from the sidelines. Ralph and I learned to play by watching them. Sometimes we'd have a game first, and then Mother or Father would play the winner. Do you play, Mildred?"

"Oh, yes! Much to my mother's shame, I love a good game of chess. I played with my brothers and then my father. Mother thought it was unladylike and didn't encourage it. Father argued that it was good for my brain." Mildred chuckled.

"It is a wonderful exercise in strategy, warfare, tactics. I am often able to work out real-life problems when I play a good game of chess."

"Tell me more about your boyhood, Fred." He needed little coaxing before he was reminiscing again.

"Ralph and I loved to build a campfire in our gum tree forest, and we'd camp out with a tent and cook over an open fire. On Sundays, we'd go shooting, and perhaps we'd bring home a duck or a rabbit, and in the summers, we'd fish. We rode our horses everywhere and could even ride them down to Dillon Beach, near our place. We loved swimming in the ocean, very bracing! Mother and Father would go and we'd fish in the surf or go clamming, we'd all go there as a family for a cook-out and play in the waves." Fred had a far-away look in his eyes and a smile that started at the corner of his mouth.

"When spring came, Ralph and I helped Father deliver the baby animals—lambs, calves, colts, and foals. If you asked my brother, he'd probably tell you that was his favorite memory."

"Seems like a wonderful way to grow up. I sense though, that a lot was expected of you, a lot of hard work."

"I suppose so. I admit when I got to Harvard and realized all I was required to do was study and learn the law, it almost felt too easy, too relaxed. Where were all the cows? Where were my duties and obligations? When I delved into my studies, I realized my priorities were different now, and would never be the same again."

"How is your father managing now that you're gone?"

"He has hired hands. It's not hard to find someone looking for that sort of work, but it can be hard to find a reliable worker."

"And your mother? Does she miss you terribly?"

"She is a Quaker. I'm sure in her way, she misses us, but I doubt she'd ever say so. She is reserved, austere."

"Were you brought up with religion?" Mildred's own family belonged to the Methodist Church but neither of her parents were particularly religious. She'd go as far as to say that her mother was too busy for church and her father was more interested in intellectual matters.

"We went to church so that we knew what it was about, but I found no comfort in it. I don't know about Ralph. Now, Father's parents, they were religious. Especially my Grandfather Parmenus. He died when I was quite young but he always frightened me with his wrathful God talk. My father did not follow the path of his father's faith. You'd think that would be troublesome in the family, but my grandfather and father had a mutual respect for one another. They didn't always see eye to eye, but it didn't seem to stop them from caring about each other and I know my father misses him and his council. Grandma Marilla died a few years ago. Ralphie and I thought she was special, a wise-woman with deep understanding gleaned from nature. She claimed my father had similar powers."

"What kind of powers?" Mildred thought she'd like to know a lot more about Marilla Woodworth.

"I don't know exactly how to describe their ways, but Father prays for good weather and happy cows, and a healthy family. He thanks the earth for its many blessings. Father says being on a pleasant green hill, looking out towards the ocean, and watching the setting sun is his church and religion. Quakers, as you may know, believe that everyone can experience the divine nature of the universe with no ritual or special leader needed to make that happen. My parents gave Ralph and me a religious upbringing, but they believed it was up to us to make our own choices. I've always appreciated their approach."

"Being from an old family with somewhat rigid beliefs, I find that refreshing."

"I don't want you to get the wrong idea about them," Fred chuckled, "my parents may have modern ideas about religion, but about everything else, they are exceedingly old-fashioned."

"Tell me more about your mother. Does she like music? Does she sing?"

Fred thought about that for a moment, with his head cocked a bit, trying to imagine. "No, I don't believe I've ever heard her sing, but Father does, and he's got quite a good voice for it. You should hear him serenade his cows. Mother played the violin when she was a girl, and she used to play a bit when Ralph and I were young before we'd go to bed. She could play beautiful, classical pieces and she knew all the old songs, too. But Father did not enjoy the sound of the violin, so she stopped. Now, she says she doesn't have the time, and it hurts her hands. She has arthritis in her fingers from working so hard her whole life."

Mildred was intrigued by Fred's stories of his parents, his family. *I would really like to meet them*, she thought and was surprised by the idea. She kept this to herself, not willing to share quite yet.

Fred was unaware of her epiphany and continued his account. "Mother loves going to the opera and the symphony, which even I find surprising. It is a rare treat, but Father takes her whenever they travel, and sometimes they go to San Francisco for a weekend with her brother, and they'll see a musical performance then. I am always surprised at how much Mother has to say about those trips. She is of the plain folk, but she craves the beauty of classical music and the operatic voices."

"Someday, maybe I can play piano for her."

Encouraged by her talk of the future, Fred exclaimed, "Oh yes! I'm sure we would all love to hear you play."

Mildred graduated from college and returned to Memphis to teach school while Fred completed his law degree.

After Fred sat for the bar exam, he traveled to Tennessee to ask for Mildred's hand in marriage. Mrs. Mathes thought he was an ambitious and likable young man. Mildred could tell her father was not entirely convinced, but in the end both agreed to the union. The young couple decided on a long engagement. It would give both opportunities to fulfill commitments they'd made—Mildred to her teaching position at the girl's school and Fred wanted time to establish himself as an attorney in San Francisco.

During the engagement, Fred and Mildred weren't able to see each other. The distance between California and Tennessee made it impossible, and every penny they could save went towards their future together. They made do with frequent, long letters back and forth, which spoke of their love and mutual dreams, and about Fred's practice, and Mildred's work and her writing.

Mildred spoke of daily life, her work with the young ladies at school, and the other teachers. She always tried to include amusing anecdotes about her parents or brothers as a way for Fred to get to know them all on a deeper level. She devoted quite a bit of time each week to creating missives that would help to keep their separation bearable.

Fred didn't seem interested in crafting the same type of experiences for Mildred. Rather, he fretted constantly about money, how much everything was costing him. There were letters steeped with negative thoughts and ideas, and Mildred had a hard time reading through them. He complained about his parents, his brother, his law practice, his finances, the state of the economy. And rarely did he tell her that she was missed. Sometimes she'd tell her family about his laments and they'd tell her to break the engagement. Those conversations became tiresome and frustrated her mightily, and she stopped sharing her predicament.

Finally, the day came when Fred sent her a letter that was so alarming she couldn't ignore there were serious problems. While Mildred didn't expect or want flowery love poems from her fiancé, she found his words difficult to accept and the level of his selfishness bizarre. She wondered if his behavior was that of a person who suffered mental difficulties or if he was simply having a bad week and it would pass. She decided to consult her mother. She had not wanted to give away any weakness on her or her fiancé's part, but after all, her parents had weathered many a marital storm.

"Mama, I've had a distressing letter from Fred." Mildred brought the letter with her into the study. Her mother was dressed to go out and sitting at her writing table, scribbling furiously.

"Daughter, tell me what is upsetting you but make it quick. I'm getting ready for the ladies' luncheon in town."

"Mama, you must listen. I don't know what I should do." Mildred unfolded the letter and began reading.

My dearest Mildred,

As the months quickly pass, I am beginning to believe that I will never accumulate enough paying clients in my practice to afford a wife, household, and children.

Your letters speak of all the places we will go and things we will do, and the pressure of your needs is a stress that I believe is unfair. When I think about the lifestyle you expect, I am left sweating and cold in the middle of the night. Those nights, by the way, when I should be resting so that I am fully prepared for my clients the following day.

I have spoken of these matters with my mother and her only response is to suggest that we call off the wedding, or at the very least, a postponement. I cannot decide which is the better path for me.

I do not want to wait forever for us to wed, but I have not saved as much money as anticipated. My account only shows a paltry sum when I had thought to have at least enough to put a reasonable down payment on a house by now.

Mildred, please think of something that will make me feel happy again and let me know right away. I write to you for your advice in the matter. Every day I fear I grow further and further from my dream of prosperity.

Fred Woodworth.

"What am I to do? Honestly, this letter makes me wonder if I'd be better off just staying here teaching my students, living the uncomplicated life of a spinster, and taking care of my loving mama and papa when they're old." Mildred said this as a joke, but the look her mother gave her told her she would not be welcome in her parents' home indefinitely.

"Mildred, you write him back this instant and tell him to shape up. He's a Harvard-educated man, an attorney; not some little boy." Mildred wondered whether Fred would respond well to being written to in this way. Perhaps it would invigorate his enthusiasm again.

"You're right, Mama."

"Consider this, Daughter: If he cannot find the money, then perhaps you *should* call the whole thing off. Be firm, and tell him you mean business. Now leave me be. I'm late, and I'm still in the middle of the notes for my speech."

She rolled her eyes at her mother's mercurial ways. "Mama, you contradict yourself and give unhelpful advice. And I thought you were going to a luncheon, not a speech."

"You knew about the luncheon with the D.A.R. Obviously, you've forgotten. And if you don't like my advice, speak with your father."

"Why wasn't I invited, Mama? I'm a member too."

"You were invited. You've been too busy carrying on with your teaching and your wedding plans. When you didn't respond, I took it upon myself to tell them you were otherwise engaged. And you are. You are most welcome."

"I am very sorry, Mama. I hope I didn't embarrass you. Please express my sincere apologies to the ladies. I'll make it up to you, I promise."

Her mother stood up quickly and gave her daughter a kiss on the forehead. "Now I really am terribly late. Do not worry, Darling. All will come out alright. You tell that young man to get hold of himself." Mildred let herself out of the study and went back up to her room to write Fred.

———✦———

As her mother suggested, Mildred invited her father to lunch near his newspaper office. Their waiter seated them and presented them with menus. As her father mulled over meal options, Mildred decided to get right to the point. "Papa, how do I know Fred is the right man for me?"

"Are you having second thoughts? What has brought this on?" She saw the worry on his face. Mildred hadn't intended to do that. He had so much on his mind already, what with Mama and her various maladies. Her handsome papa looked tired, pained. Mildred surmised his leg, that had been amputated mid-thigh, must have been bothering him. He wore a prosthetic device over the stump, and it rubbed and hurt him, but he never complained.

"I assumed Mama had told you about my concerns."

"She has not." At that moment, the waiter returned and they both ordered the chicken.

As soon as they had some privacy, Mildred continued. "Fred sent me a letter stating that he feared his ability to keep me in the manner to which I have become accustomed. I take it to mean he hasn't saved much money and doesn't feel he can afford a wife, a home, and a family. Tell me the truth, is my upkeep outrageous?"

Her father shrugged, "By my accounting, you've never asked for frivolous things."

"I think you're being too kind. You know I've asked for dresses and parties, and my education was very expensive."

"Mildred, be honest, did you actually ask for those things, or did your mother insist? She has certain expectations, you know." He looked at his daughter and she had to agree with what he said. It had mostly been to make her mother happy. When unhappy, Mama was impossible to live with. Not that she was ever easy when things went her way. Mildred chuckled to herself.

"Of course, college was not part of her plan, but I was delighted to provide you with a higher education. Your studies, your books, your music—those were the things that mattered to you."

———✦———

J. Harvey was devastated to know he was about to lose his only daughter to the wilds of California. Father and daughter were of similar personality, and she'd always been more like a trusted friend than his child. He knew a parent was supposed to love all his children equally, but in his eyes, Mildred was special. Truth be told, she possessed a rare and exceptional mind.

Indeed, he pondered, *was Fred a good match for Mildred? Only time would tell.*

Their food arrived, and the next few minutes were silent as they enjoyed the delicious fare before continuing their conversation.

Mildred pushed her plate away. "Thank you, Papa, that was delicious." She couldn't eat another thing.

"You're welcome. Coffee and dessert?" he asked.

"Maybe, just a little." Mildred laughed, as she'd just declared herself full. "Papa, you know I have to marry a smart man and Fred is intelligent. We talk about everything! The world, politics, his career, my writing, my obsession with our family lineage. Anything I could possibly think of to talk about, he can go on and on about it, too! And Papa, he's handsome. His dark hair and flashing silvery eyes are divine."

"That's enough. I don't want to hear about how attractive your young man is. It is the quality of the character of the man that is important, not how he looks. Pick a different topic immediately, Daughter." He laughed softly. *Maybe she was more like her mother than he'd ever realized.*

"You know, he's also sensitive and thoughtful. I like that in anyone, but in a man, I find it unusual and attractive." J. Harvey looked at his daughter with raised eyebrows but didn't interrupt her. "When he discusses the law, he's like a wolf that will not stop until his prey is utterly devoured. Recently though, his letters seem to show that he's lost his confidence. This worries me."

"Every young man loses a bit of swagger when they realize they're responsible for themselves the very first time. I was much the same. I thought I knew it all, and when it was demonstrated that the exact opposite was true, it came as a shock. Eventually, thank goodness, I learned the importance of being humble."

"Hmm," she said. "I think Fred has much to learn about the subject of humility."

"A tough lesson and perhaps part of his current struggle, don't you think?" her father smiled patiently.

"You must be right."

"What kind of couple will you be? Will you be partners and make important decisions together, or will he insist on being the one in charge? Now this is my opinion, but I think if he's smart, he'll consult you on all important matters."

"I suppose I had imagined that we'd be equal partners. Wouldn't you think so, Papa? Come to think of it, how do you and Mama navigate such things?"

"Your mother and I both have our strengths and our weaknesses. I'm not sure if I'd call our marriage one that is always equal, but I will say that I have sought her counsel many times, and more often than not, I have sided with her opinion. There were times when we were vehemently opposed, or do you not remember her response when you announced you were going to attend Vassar? But we've always listened to each other with open minds and open hearts. My dear, you had better find out how Fred feels about equality before you are married. Not every man wants a partner with such great strength. My advice to you is to have a long and honest discussion with Fred Woodworth regarding this topic and do it quickly!"

"Of course, you are right as always, Papa. I have to know that my opinions will be considered in all decisions we make as husband and wife. On that topic, I will not bend."

Her father chuckled, "You are a formidable opponent and an invaluable ally. Which will you be in your marriage?"

"He will not want me as an adversary," she replied.

"Daughter, you are too bold by half."

"Where do you think I learned it, Papa? You taught me well. And of course, I've got Mama's sense of the dramatic. You both made me the person I am, and for that, I am *mostly* grateful," Mildred quipped.

"And I am so very proud of you, Daughter. Now talk to Fred and tell him what he can expect in a marriage with Mildred Overton Mathes. You are a rare treasure, my girl. Do not ever lose yourself, and do not forget who you are."

"Papa, you always know just what to say. Thank you for being the best father and friend." She leaned over and gave J. Harvey a kiss on the cheek just as the waiter set down their dessert—peaches and cream.

Chapter Sixteen
Conversation with Abby

What has startled me awake? My heart pounds in my ears, and I know I'm not alone in this unfamiliar room. Standing before the hearth and a roaring fire is my great-great-grandmother, Abigail. Her back rigid, hands clasped, the essence of control.

"You are but a dream," I insist softly. She turns to me and frowns. "Surely you cannot feel the cold."

"Death allows its little rituals. And I do as I wish. In my time, I craved the heat. It soothed my lungs and warmed my aches." She looks around the room and seems to recognize where she is. There is a look of satisfaction and a momentary longing.

"Where is this place, Grandmother? Is this The Tomales?" I ask. I smell wood smoke and mustiness and dirt and melancholy. Perhaps it is an echo from her grave.

"It is the house where I grew up. In the East," she answers.

"The East," I repeat. "Why did you bring me here?"

She is irritable. "There is familiarity of my old home in Neversink. I desired that comfort. Would you deny me? Why must young people be so self-centered?"

Am I sparring with her? "Of course not and I'm hardly a youngster. Nevertheless, I am younger than you, so I'll give you that."

"You are impertinent as well as selfish. Now, let me enjoy my fire."

"Do as you wish, Grandmother."

The air surrounding us shimmers and I find myself curled up on a dusty settee stuffed with horsehair and springs that were determined to poke through. Has she covered me with an old quilt? She must have because I am quiet cozy here. She has performed an act of caring that comes as a surprise. Abby is still at the hearth, and I feel the heat of the fire and her stare.

She is silent for a few seconds, deciding. "I thought we should meet since you are bent on telling my secrets. You seem to have a fair sense of how it was. An objective view. I suppose the letters helped. We were concerned about those."

"The family." Of course, there is no question in my mind, still I am determined to verify.

"Yes," she replies. "We thought everything might be lost. No one could remember where to find those trunks. There was always the possibility the letters would burn in a fire or be lost in a flood, but they were not, and you found them."

"If you're daughter-in-law hadn't been so careful, I never would have. But I still have questions. Will you tell me about Mildred and Fred? Tell me how things were." Have I asked the impossible?

What I asked for doesn't seem to bother her, and we sit for a minute, together, before she begins telling me about my great-grandparents when they were young and in love.

Fred & Mildred (Mathes) Woodworth

(1869 – 1908) (1870 – Living)

|

Hall

(1898 – 1941)

Benjamin

(1900 – Living)

Harvey

(1901 – 1928)

Mildred (Millie)

(1903 – Living)

Phyllis

(1908 – Living)

Chapter Seventeen
Wedded Bliss

Nearly two years after announcing their engagement, Fred and Mildred were married on June 16, 1897 at Mt. Olive Methodist Church in Memphis. The reception was immediately following at J. Harvey's home.

Several weeks after Fred's alarming letting, he wrote back to Mildred in apology.

> ...*please forgive my outburst, Mildred, I was so worried about our lives together, but I know we can make it work. Please say you'll forgive me.*

She forgave him wholeheartedly. Her mama was relieved but Papa and her brothers were not altogether convinced.

Mildred's parents gave them an elaborate wedding party steeped in family tradition. Fred was delighted by the illusion of wealth, even for just one afternoon. He looked over at the table laden with gifts and thought he'd never seen such abundance, such finery.

He was disappointed that his parents hadn't attended, but considering the distance, not surprised. Besides, he was sure they would have been quite uncomfortable with the ostentatious display and formality. He could not imagine his father in this place and his mother would have been appalled by these Southerners.

Mildred and Fred sat at the head table watching the day play out. One of the wedding guests made their way over to wish them a long and happy married life, some distant relative of the Mathes family. Fred took a moment to calculate possibilities—he was on the brink of greatness. He grabbed Mildred's hand under the table and squeezed. As always, she was lovely.

"Are you enjoying yourself?" she asked. She looked hopeful.

"Most definitely. I will have to watch my intake of spirits, Mildred, I am not accustomed to it." It was somewhat of a shock to realize that nearly everyone in attendance was drinking spirits and a strangeness descended upon the revelry as wine was consumed in quantity that seemed to lead to a mass relaxing of jaw muscles and behavior in the lazy heat of the afternoon. If food was not served quickly, Fred feared there might be trouble.

The back of his neck felt warm and prickly under the close scrutiny of Mildred's family. Throughout the day, he was sure he'd heard whispers of Yankee or Yank but he tried not to let it bother him. He supposed it was a fair assessment as his mother was from New York.

It was possible that some of Mildred's previous suitors were in attendance today; he had not asked. He knew how these old families operated; they were all very closely connected. But, it was the young attorney from California who'd married the daughter of one of Memphis' leading families, not any of these Southern boys. He silently congratulated himself.

Succulent roast pork, baked apples, candied yams, fried okra, dishes of greens, plates of sliced melon, and ripe berry delights were heaped on gleaming serving platters on tables covered with snowy white linen. The scent of gardenias wafted on the warm breeze brought in through open floor-to-ceiling windows. Flowers cascaded out of dozens of vases or rested languidly in delicate crystal bowls. A string quartet could be heard from the ballroom were dancing would be held later. Dinner was served and it was divine.

Every guest held up their flutes of champagne as one reveler making a toast finished his speech, and another took over the duty. There was much good humor and laughter in the crowd. Fred noticed that Mildred's mother was entirely at home in society, while her father appeared bored with the formality.

J. Harvey, as everyone called him, mainly seemed amused by the guests but as he locked eyes with his son-in-law, a dangerous feeling passed between them. At that moment, Mildred got her father's attention and he gave her a quick smile, not quite a happy one, more of a smile that remembered happy times long gone. She smiled back through the crowd. "Thank you, Papa."

Fred was the outsider. Except for a few mutual friends from Harvard and, of course, Ralph, he had no one else representing him from his side of the family. At first, he hadn't been bothered by the deficit, but now that the reception was in full swing, he felt the need for his people. After all, it was his day as well as Mildred's, and he deserved a good portion of the attention as well.

The Secret Lives of Ancestors

Ralph wandered over to where Fred stood on the edge of the room observing the day.

"Brother, you look very well turned out," he complimented. "And your bride is a beautiful queen."

"Of course, Ralph. It is my wedding day. How else would I be?" Fred waited for his younger brother to find some fault.

"Don't be so defensive. The Mathes family has given you a wonderful beginning to your marriage and I wish you both all the luck in the world."

"It's a pity that Mildred's father is so standoffish and her brothers as well. I don't understand it. They should embrace me with open arms."

"You mean like Mother will embrace Mildred?" Ralph scoffed.

"Stop trying to ruin my day." Fred abandoned his brother and their conversation. He met Mildred in the middle of the dance floor as the first dance was announced.

Fred felt confident as he led his wife through the waltz. Of course, Mildred was completely at ease as she had been doing these kinds of things her entire life. Then her father cut in and as they danced Fred took a turn with Mildred's mother. She did not speak through the entire dance, but Fred could see J. Harvey and his daughter speak animatedly.

Finally, Mildred danced with all of her brothers and while she did, Fred went to the edge of the ballroom and watched. She was radiantly happy, especially with her youngest brother. *I could never feel this at ease with my family,* he thought. He admitted he was a bit jealous of the manner in which Mildred conducted herself.

Fred felt a definite friction with Mildred's brothers. He'd never spoken about anything but the insurance business with Lee—as soon as Fred tried to move to other matters, Lee saw someone he needed to speak with and walked away. J. Harvey, Jr., who was Mildred's favorite, had wild eyes and a restless spirit and Fred could honestly say he was a bit afraid of him. He couldn't tell what Ben and Talbot thought except that they'd pointedly told him that they'd hoped their sister would marry someone from their social circle. *Thank goodness we'll not have much to do with the Mathes boys.*

"Fred, will you please join me as I say goodbye to our guests?" asked Mildred.

"Certainly. The day just flew by, didn't it? Are you happy, my Darling?" he asked.

"Yes, Fred, I am content." Mildred smiled lovingly at her husband. He'd done well today but she could tell it had not been easy for him.

They honeymooned near Chattanooga at Lookout Mountain, enjoying the beautiful views and fresh air. Mildred was a good sport and accompanied him on daily hikes for views of the river and the Tennessee Valley below. In evenings, they read and played chess and talked about their future together in California. They found contentment in this quiet place that seemed to soothe both of them.

On his way home to California, Fred felt their idyll begin to slip away. It made him nervous, queasy to contemplate Mildred meeting his parents, especially his mother. He tried to solidify in his mind how things might go, but the picture remained hazy at best. Fred was sure his father would get along fine with Mildred and be won over by her intelligence and beauty. In turn, his wife would like Abijah Woodworth. He had a fine sense of humor that she would find charming. But what would his mother think? No matter how he tried, Fred couldn't imagine. It was his hope that the two women would become fast friends. *After all*, he thought, *they are both highly educated, strong women, and teachers. Couldn't that be a basis for harmony?* He prayed all would be well.

The train ride home was uncomfortable and her husband was plagued with an upset stomach and constant headaches for most of the journey. Mildred noticed and tried to pry the problem from him, which made him cranky and short with her.

"Please leave me to myself. I'm unwell and there's nothing you can do about it." He could be so infantile when things didn't go as he planned.

"I'm sorry you're ill." She turned away from him and gazed out the window. He'd been rude, but made no move to make apologies.

While Fred was sullenly nursing another headache, Mildred watched the miles go by from their private compartment. She thought back to the wedding, their reception, their honeymoon. Her parents made the day perfect in every way for her and certainly Fred had seemed impressed. He'd chosen the honeymoon and that had been fine with her. Her only requirement was something away from the hustle and bustle of her everyday life and Lookout Mountain was certainly that.

Mildred felt her cheeks heat as she remembered their wedding night which was a complete disappointment. Not that she'd had anything to compare it to, but she had read love stories, and thought there would be some basic tenderness to the thing. Mama didn't prepare her for her obligations as a wife and she was *still* angry with her for that.

For his part, Fred didn't seem to know what he was about either, and the entire act felt demeaning to Mildred—filled with perspiration and the knocking of noses and bones and misplaced elbows. It was messy and wet and made her wish she could take a long, hot bath in complete privacy. It was wholly without grace and she could only hope that as they became more accustomed to one another that things would improve. When Fred had finished with a grunt, she watched horrified, as he turned away from her and within moments was snoring so loudly she feared the neighbors would complain. *Shouldn't it be less terrible? Less humiliating?* It seemed a strange thing to pray about, but she considered it and wished desperately for someone in which she could confide.

Although the similarities were solid, the differences between his family and his wife's were vast. Fred was going over pros and cons, perhaps something he should have done before they married.

The biggest issue, Fred saw, was that his mother was a staunch abolitionist, but Mildred had been born at the end of the Civil War in Memphis and was a Southern Belle. Fred's family had started from the bottom and had created a successful business. They were not wealthy but they were well off and had money to do the things they wanted to do. Mildred's family lived in relative luxury accumulated from generations of dead relatives. They employed servants to do the cooking and cleaning and take care of their every need. His father was from pioneer stock and a bit rough around the edges. Her father was a journalist, a newspaperman, and had been a Captain in the Confederate Army.

Upon speaking with Mildred's father, Fred learned that the man was not a soldier at heart. He had no love of the War or anything to do with it. Despite his personal feelings, when the time came, J. Harvey fulfilled his obligation to the Confederate Army and served with distinction. Fred supposed her father's loyalty could be commended, but wished fervently that J. Harvey wasn't so public about his deeds. Mildred's mother was very proud of her husband's service, loved to see him in his uniform, and quite liked the role of being a Captain's wife.

"Maybe Mother doesn't need to know about your father's role in the Confederacy." Mildred looked dumbstruck by his comment.

"However I feel about the Confederacy, what is not in question is my pride for my father's service. I think it's wrong to try to hide who we are as a family." Her expression told Fred that she would not back down where her parents were concerned.

Because of what she had witnessed growing up after the War, Mildred had very definite ideas about rights and equality for all men and women. She was very vocal in her beliefs, but would that be enough to win over Fred's mother? He wondered if the Quaker woman from New York could ever trust anyone from the South, even if the Southerner was her daughter-in-law.

They were a few short hours from completing their train travel when Fred finally spoke of his plans. "I want you to see The Tomales, just for a few days, and of course meet my parents. I hope that's alright with you."

" I'm excited to meet your family."

"I'm sure they will be pleased to meet you, never fear. Then it's on to San Raphael to see our new home!" Fred was perspiring fiercely in the summer heat, and his discomfort was clear to see. His bride looked cool and calm. He wondered how she managed to appear so composed and told her so, only to have her tell him how she really felt.

"Fred, I hope they like me. I've been so worried. Especially about being a Southerner."

"Do you smell the salt air? Now I know I'm truly home." Finally, Mildred heard some excitement in Fred's voice.

Mildred loved how clean everything smelled. The coastal breezes were invigorating and felt so different from her home and even from New York. She hoped they'd be able to go to the ocean to dip toes into the surf. She wanted to feel the ocean waves.

But for now, she wanted to stop and wash away the weariness of their journey. "Are we almost there?" Fred nodded. "I do hope they like me. I keep going over and over in my mind what it will be like to be their daughter-in-law. I will try not to make any mistakes." Mildred smiled a little but was twisting her handkerchief in her fingers.

"There it is. The house on the hill!" Suddenly she wished the journey wasn't over yet.

Her first glimpse of the property where her husband spent his childhood revealed an impressive driveway lined on either side by mature eucalyptus trees. The couple bumped and jolted to the top of the hill in the little buggy. On the left were two large barns, a bunkhouse, and a half dozen smaller sheds and corrals. On the right was an expanse of rich green grass and fencing that separated the pasture where sheep and cows grazed in the midday sun. At the top of the hill was a large white ranch house. It was simple in design but still included the beautiful Queen Anne architectural details that made the home unique. It was much grander than Mildred had imagined.

"Fred, what a beautiful home! Your father designed it himself?"

"Yes, he did. Be sure to compliment him; he's very proud of it."

Standing to the right of the front door stood a short, stout woman, with arms crossed over her breasts. Perfectly rigid, she stared straight ahead. Abby Woodworth wore a stern expression, and she exuded strength. Her grey hair was worn in a tight knot of compliance on top of her head. Her dress was entirely unadorned, and the dark grey fabric looked as though it had been washed many times. Mildred felt a distinct chill and shivered.

On horseback, a few feet away from where Fred brought the buggy to a stop, was Abijah. He wore a dark grey coat and vest, and his trousers were tucked into mud-crusted work boots. Tilted low over his eyes was a dusty old Homburg and a faded kerchief was tied at his neck. After a few moments, Abijah dismounted and moved to help his daughter-in-law down from the carriage.

"Welcome, Daughter! Welcome to The Tomales. Hello there, Fred, welcome home."

The three made their way to where Abby stood, and Fred made introductions.

"I'd like to introduce my wife, Mildred Overton Mathes Woodworth."

Fred smiled brightly, but the sweat dripped down his face.

"Hello there, Mr. and Mrs. Woodworth. I am so pleased to make your acquaintance." Mildred dipped a proper curtsy as she grasped at the proffered hand of Abijah, and he gave it a little squeeze and winked at her. Then she walked up to Abby and executed the same curtsy and handshake. Mildred searched her mother-in-law's face for a sign of welcome but sensed only unwavering intensity.

"Fred, what is she saying? I can't understand a word of it," said his mother in her clipped Eastern tones.

"Mother, Mildred says she's pleased to meet you." Fred translated. He was red in the face, and Mildred could tell he was embarrassed, but with his wife or his mother, she wasn't sure.

Abby was unmoved. Her look said she'd judged Mildred, and found her lacking. "Your accent is very strong; it's almost as though you're not speaking English."

"Mrs. Woodworth, I'm so sorry. I will just have to learn how to speak more slowly." Mildred wanted to run away and cry, but she couldn't.

"Well, your accent is as thick and difficult to understand spoken slowly as quickly, so never mind. I expect I'll have to adjust." Mildred didn't believe Abby had any intention of adapting. She looked to Fred for encouragement, but he looked down, fascinated with his shoes and probably wishing they'd never left Memphis.

"Come to the dining room, children. Abby's prepared a meal for us." Abijah tried to get things back on course.

The dinner, comprised of plain, hearty food from their garden and ranch, was seasoned with awkward pauses, and conversation did not flow comfortably. Mildred hesitated to say more than a few words at a time, and each time she did, Abby screwed up her face and shook her head as though the act of listening was too painful. Her mother-in-law objected to her; the southern drawl just made things more difficult. She'd wager that had Abby approved of her, the accent would have made no difference.

"Fred tells me your father fought in the Confederate Army." *Here we go.* "Did he tell you that I am a Yankee, born and bred in New York? Did he tell you that I loathe the Confederacy and all it stands for?"

Oh boy, now were in it, Abijah thought. His wife spoke in a rapid-fire of words while serving coffee and apple pie. He watched his daughter-in-law, blushing and ashamed; her eyes filled with tears and threatened to overflow.

Too late, Fred came to his wife's aid. "Mother, must we discuss this tonight?"

"Yes, Abby, let's leave talk of politics and war for another time. I can tell the children are exhausted. At least let them have a good-night's sleep before the roasting begins." Abijah tried to ease Abby out of her temper with a bit of humor, but she looked at him and scowled.

Fred got up abruptly from the dining table and helped Mildred up too. "We are going to bed."

"Thank you, Mrs. Woodworth, for the delicious dinner," said Mildred quietly, unwilling to meet Abby's stare. Fred pulled her from the scene abruptly, tugging at her arm to hurry her away from his mother's focus.

They made their way up the stairs to the bedroom Fred and Ralph shared as boys. The twin beds were covered in brown and gray quilts. There was a short bookshelf placed between the beds, and Mildred spied a collection of books about mountain climbing, Tennyson's poetry, and a few volumes of Shakespeare. On the opposite wall, was a rectangular painting with a lovely gilt frame. It was of a man fishing at dusk on an alpine lake. Fred noticed her looking at it. "My brother

Ralph's the artist. The painting depicts one of our favorite fishing spots near Mount Shasta."

"Is that you?"Mildred asked. She tried to regain her equilibrium.

"I think so, although he never came out and said it. Maybe it's a little bit of both of us."

"It's quite a good painting. He's talented."

"Mildred, tomorrow will be different, I promise." Fred tried to sound encouraging, but it came out weak, and she heard his uncertainty.

"I am completely mortified. I don't know what I did wrong, but I must try to fix things between your mother and me." The bride from Tennessee was utterly exhausted and disappointed.

"It was not your fault. Perhaps I should have prepared you more fully for Mother's feelings about the South." He had seen his mother bring strong men to their knees with just a look. How would his genteel wife fare under the Quaker's scrutiny?

"Can that young lady milk a cow or mend a fence?" Abby wailed at Abijah that night after dinner. His wife was furiously doing dishes at the kitchen sink and chipped the edge of a serving bowl.

"No need to take it out on the dinnerware, Abby. And remember, you couldn't do those things either when we first wed." She glared at her husband before continuing her tirade.

"I tell you, she is going to cost this family a fortune in clothing and parties and frivolous things. Does she think she'll have servants? Our son has his career to think of, and she will drag him down."

"Shush, the children will hear you. You must give her a chance. I know she's young, but she's intelligent, and she will learn how we do things here, you'll see."

"Ha! Once again, you've been taken in by a pretty face! She's been indulged her entire life. Doesn't know how to cook. How is that possible? No good will come from their marriage; you mark my words." When Abby got an idea in her head, sometimes she had to wear herself out before seeing sense.

"Wife, you made your feelings very plain at dinner. I don't think you had any intention of giving her a chance, and I will say it right out, you are unfair!" Abijah shook his head sadly.

Ignoring her husband's remarks, she continued, "How can a person believe someone so polite, ridiculously so, and that accent, impossible."

"I think her accent is lovely." Abby glared at him but he continued. "She's a charming young lady and of good breeding."

She didn't answer but took a cloth and scrubbed at the kitchen table so hard, Abijah was afraid she'd get splinters.

"Enough. Go to bed and get some rest. I'll finish up here. Let's pray for better dispositions tomorrow, shall we?" It was small comfort getting the last word in with that woman.

Abby stomped off to bed, leaving Abijah with the rest of the dirty dishes and half an apple pie calling his name. Did he dare?

The following morning, everyone seemed to be in a better mood. Mildred and Fred went to breakfast together. Abijah was reading the *Petaluma Argus* newspaper, and Abby was still in the kitchen getting breakfast ready.

"Good morning, Mr. Woodworth," Mildred said with a tentative smile.

"Good morning, Daughter. Help yourself to coffee on the sideboard. Good morning, Son. I trust you slept well?"

"Yes, hello, Father. We slept well enough. Have you already been out to the barns?"

"Of course. Bossies don't care if company comes, I was up with them at three this morning, and our men were already milking. The ladies are producing nicely, and we've got a lovely batch of calves coming right along."

Abby made several trips from the kitchen with steaming containers of scrambled eggs, a huge pot of oatmeal, fried ham and potatoes, hot biscuits and gravy, and strawberry preserves.

"Eat it while it's hot. Help yourselves," she said, and went back to the kitchen to retrieve a pitcher of fresh milk and a dish of butter. She set both on the table with a bang and sat down. "We are not so formal here as you may be expecting."

"Oh, no, Mrs. Woodworth, we often have a breakfast buffet. When my brothers were still at home, breakfast was always a rushed and rather chaotic affair. My father and I always liked to linger and visit over our coffee, and Mother stays in bed sometimes until...well, never mind." Mildred stopped her rambling abruptly when she saw the look on Abby's face. "My apologies, I do go on; thank you, Mrs. Woodworth, for this wonderful breakfast. It smells divine."

"Mildred, you better fill up your plate, or it will all be cold," Fred coached.

"There's plenty, girl, don't be shy," said Abijah.

"My goodness, this is delicious, but surely the four of us aren't going to eat all of this food?" asked Mildred.

"Certainly not," Abby scoffed. "The ranch hands will come soon for theirs. They got started at three this morning."

"My wife gets up before the hands arrive and sets out a pot of oatmeal for them."

"Mrs. Woodworth, you were up so early!" Mildred exclaimed.

"It is my duty. We demand the men work hard for us, and they expect to be fed well. It is part of the agreement. Mr. Woodworth was up milking cows just as early. It is the life of a dairy farmer."

"And they will do it all over again this afternoon at three and work until eight in the evening," Fred added.

"Then, at least, while we are here, please allow me to help by cleaning up after the meals," Mildred offered shyly.

"That would be a help. Yes, you may do the dishes," Abby allowed.

"Wife, I thought I'd show Mildred around the property this morning," said Abijah.

"You can wait until the kitchen work is done. I'm sure you and your son have much to discuss."

The remainder of the meal was spent in relative peace and quiet until the hired men arrived. They made their quiet greetings, sat down at the opposite end of the table, and systematically devoured the rest of the food. The exhausted men didn't partake in much conversation, just occasional low murmuring questions and replies about the cows. With a quick "Thank you, Mrs. W." they returned to the bunkhouse until the afternoon milking.

"Mildred, did you eat enough? Our men didn't leave so much as a crumb. I managed to hold back a couple of biscuits. We might need them before noon."

"Oh, thank you, Fred. I was too nervous to eat a thing. Your mother watched me like a hawk."

"Yes, she's like that. She always knew what my brother and I were up to. We didn't get away with much," Fred chuckled. "Say, that was an excellent idea about helping in the kitchen. Be sure to ask her exactly how she wants things done, though. Mother is very particular."

"I had already guessed."

Fred's law practice became well known in affluent circles as he and Mildred entertained the cream of San Francisco society. This lifestyle was very costly and he went back again and again to his mother for subsidy that she blamed on Mildred.

He worked long hours in San Francisco while Mildred made their home in San Rafael a place he was proud of. Fred rented a small apartment near his office; it was much more efficient than for him to make the daily commute.

On rare days off, the Woodworth's held dinner parties or went to the theater, and occasionally they picnicked in Golden Gate Park or went to the ocean to watch the waves roll in. It was a busy time in their marriage but a sweet time.

From the outside, Fred's marriage seemed perfect. Mildred was clever and cordial and always willing to listen to him speak of his future as a prosperous attorney. He enjoyed their time together as brief as it was. If only he could make his mother more cooperative.

Your wife is a spendthrift. She'll have you in the poorhouse before you know it. His mother's words echoed irritatingly in Fred's brain. He'd done what he could to placate her, but never explained that he was the one who needed the money. It served his story that Abby should think Mildred was responsible for expenses incurred and he never stood up for his wife.

Chapter Eighteen
Conversation with Mildred

The garden table is set for tea. My great-grandmother, Mildred, sits across from me gazing contentedly at the enormous blue and purple hydrangea blooms. It's lovely and warm today, and the scent of roses lingers sweetly.

She's in her thirties and is beautiful with kind eyes and a thoughtful expression. Her dress is tidy, but I see many gathers and seams have been taken in and let out. She has made it over many times, as her body swelled and then diminished with the birth of each child. Her hands are red and cracked from washing clothes by hand and digging in her garden. The tips of her thumb and fingers on her right hand are stained blue. I surmise she'd been writing late at night in secret after the rest of the household sleeps.

A pot of tea steeps, and I've put out a plate of biscuits, with a crock of butter and a jar of honey with a wooden dipper. I understand these are just props, but it seems more civilized and genteel for two ladies to visit over a proper tea.

"Thank you for agreeing to our visit, Granny."

"Of course, Sugah. And before you ask, we all know about the book," she replies in her soft drawl, leaning in towards me intently as she smoothes the table cloth to keep her hands busy. "And, I want to help you."

"If I ask you something you don't wish to speak of, please tell me," I coach.

"I'm ready to part with every little thing I know. You'll do right by us, we know that." Granny looks down into her cup. Perhaps she is searching the tea leaves for our fortunes, our hidden truths.

AMYLEE

I push a photograph of me as a toddler toward her. She is in the photo with me along with my mother and my nana. "Do you remember this Granny? You would have been 97 or 98 years old in it."

"Sakes alive, yes, I remember. You were such a little thing. We were here, weren't we?"

I nod my reply then continue. "I was told that when you held me on your lap that day, you said I'd be the one to tell the family stories. Is that true?"

"Of course, it's true. We all know about you, and you agreed before you were even born. The writing is your life's work. I began the work, and others in the family have added to it, but I think you will be the one to finish it." Granny smiles at me. "But, a story like ours will never be completely finished, will it?"

"Our story is long, is it not? And I'll do my best with it."

"Where shall we begin?"

I breathe in deeply and let it out, centering myself. "Tell me about your mother. What was she like?"

"Oh goodness, my mama," Granny laughs. "She was a handful. Very dramatic. And she loved her spirits, a bit more than she should. Spoiled, I'd say, by her grandfather and her father and then by my father.

"Mama just had to be the center of attention. She never came right out and said, but I always felt she was jealous of Papa and me. We were close. Mama wasn't what I'd call a deep thinker, but she was clever and had a near-perfect memory for names and places. She knew everyone in Memphis society and aspired to be at the top rung of the ladder. She was very politically opinionated and a true daughter of the old South. Papa and I had our ideas about what the South should be, and Mama leaned in the opposite direction. She was happy with Shelby County being the center of her universe.

"She did come to visit me in California, but I always had the idea she didn't feel comfortable out here. It was not her world. 'Too much space and not enough polite company,' she said. 'And your ocean, it's just so big and overstated.' Of course, she'd never been to the ocean before. She simply could not fathom the depths."

"Did your mother have the same passion for genealogy as you?"

"She did not. She wanted to know how the different family members were connected, especially if the ancestor was historically significant or wealthy. Politicians, landowners, founding fathers, those sorts. She wanted to be kept apprised of those kinds of discoveries. But only so she could brag about it with her ladies' groups. And, of course, for the *Daughters of the American Revolution*. To be invited to join, you have to prove your lineage to a patriot." There is a pause in the conversation, and I refill my cup. Granny's tea remains untouched.

"How did you get interested in genealogy?" I ask.

"I was fascinated with history and world affairs from Papa and then later at Vassar, but my interest in our family history came from Mama's sister, my Aunt Ella. Ella and Mama were not close, but I liked her tremendously."

I continue the questioning, moving on to the subject of my great-grandfather. "What did your mother think of Fred?"

"Oh, she liked him well enough. Smart, handsome, Harvard Law School, well educated, and he seemed to come from money. Of course, he was from California, a Yankee, but that couldn't be helped, could it? The Woodworth family had been in America since the sixteen hundreds. Their lineage is at least as interesting as the Mathes family. Mama would have liked Fred to be a bit more established, you know, with more in the way of assets, but Fred was just getting started, and I loved him. Upon meeting him, she told me that he was a braggart and a bit too sure of himself, but that wasn't necessarily a negative in her eyes."

"Would she have been happier if you'd chosen a man from the South, perhaps?" I ask.

"Yes. I had other prospects, wealthy young men from respectable old families, but they were dull. They were not interested in my ideas or opinions. And honestly, Sugah, I didn't care about theirs," she says.

"And Fred was interested in what you thought?"

"Oh, yes! Well, at least at the beginning he appeared to be. We had the most wonderful conversations about every topic in the world. We so enjoyed scouring the newspapers for articles of interest and then debating for hours. I was sure Fred and Papa would have a lot to talk about, but they didn't seem to hit it off. My father kept Fred at arm's length, never let him into his confidence. He was perfectly kind and hospitable to my husband, but I knew he didn't approve, and I think Fred guessed how Papa felt. No, he never fully trusted or accepted him. My brothers didn't care much for Fred, either. After a while, I began to understand their objections."

"Tell me about your children," I coax.

"Oh, my precious children. We were blessed. First came Hall. His was an *en caul* birth—that's very rare. Legend says they are lucky children who will never drown. He had beautiful red hair and as he got older it became darker. He was a very active child.

"Next came my Benny. He was such a happy baby. All smiles and a delight. Then came Harvey and the boys loved him so. Fred was a very proud Papa of his three boys.

"But tragedy struck when Harvey was a toddler. He fell from the wagon and sustained a serious head injury. Eventually he healed, but Lord knows, he was never right again."

I knew about Harvey and wanted more information if I could get it. "Did you ever suspect anything else troubled him, besides the head injury?"

"Oh, yes. Abby and I had many discussions about the poor child. Harvey could be the sweetest angel you could ever imagine and then in a flash he was angry, violent even. The poor dear was trapped inside himself.

"Then my Millie was born. I was so excited to have a girl. By this time, Fred was becoming distant from the family. There was constant strife between him and his mother. And by the time Phyllis came...well, we'll talk about that more another time."

"I wish you could stay, Granny. Will you please come back again?"

"I'll come back, Granddaughter, but now I must go."

I want to hug her. To feel the love that I felt as a little girl. I want that safety, that security.

"I love you, Granny. Goodbye."

"Love you too, Sugah."

Epilogue

After years of working on this book, I'd reached a point and needed more information on my ancestors. I was sure the stories existed, but I couldn't seem to uncover them. I was stuck.

Enter, my husband's step-sister, a Board Certified Clinical Hypnotherapist. I explained the problem, and she thought she could help. Susan specializes in Past Life Regression and Speaking with the Dead. She suggested I start with a session where she would guide me through "Speaking with the Dead."

Susan asked that I remain open to many different possibilities and outcomes. "Our session may not happen as you expect, and you may not get answers in the ways you would think."

I wasn't sure what to expect, but I hoped to learn something that would help me uncover more of the family stories.

The session began with Susan taking me through visualizing and relaxing my whole body. I was awake but in a sort of half-dream state. The image of a crowd of people flashed in my mind. It seemed like a painting, but it felt alive. The people were dressed in long black robes. Their faces were pale and almost transparent. Covering most of their faces was a rectangular, black card. There was a soft, restless murmuring of voices, and I could feel them inhaling and exhaling deeply in unison. And then, a second image revealed itself. It was an old, stylized pen and ink drawing in blue, brown, and purple of a tall ship with many masts crossing through the waves of a turbulent ocean. Although I knew this was just an image in my mind, it felt so real I was ready to climb aboard and sail across the sea.

Next, I was guided through a portal into what Susan called the inter-life. "It is the place where spirits go after death." There, I found my mother, who had passed in 2015, waiting for me.

I'm in a wooded area with mom and a soft light emanates from us. I was in that place with my mother and yet still back in Susan's office under hypnosis. I was aware of these things occurring simultaneously. The duality was distracting at first.

My mother was the conduit between myself and anyone else who would appear. Her energy was a palpable thing. It's a knowingness that she's with me.

"Tell me where you are and what's happening," Susan prompts.

"We're in the clearing in the forest, and there's a light. Behind the trees on all sides, there are a lot of shadows, people. "They are the same figures I'd seen earlier. I think they came to be with me. They are family, but I'm not sure which ones. They have awakened in this strange place, and I feel their confusion."

Susan assured us that we were in a safe place, and this settled everyone. After a few minutes, I feel my grandmother's energy, my nana.

"Talk to your ancestors, invite them to speak with you."

I tell the ancestors I want to know them. The crowd parts, and my mother's grandfather steps forward. It is Fred Woodworth. I ask him to tell me about himself. "He is showing me images of himself as a young man at school. He's bent over a desk; he must be young, with no mustache and beard yet. He is very handsome and earnest."

Fred continues to show me images of himself, and I'm surprised at how much fondness I feel for him.

I ask him again what happened, and he doesn't answer me, but I can feel the feelings he's trying to convey. He put the idea in my mind that he wanted to be a good man. Soft and free from worry. When he was in school, he wanted to do the right thing, but his life became too much for him. His mother, his wife, his children—they placed too much pressure on him.

The inside of his mind, his thoughts are complete chaos. He's depressed. His thoughts make him ill.

"Go with the emotions and keep allowing him to show you pictures," Susan coaxed.

"I can feel that he didn't know how to get out of the mess he found himself in. He was so driven to succeed, no matter the consequences."

"How did you die?" I asked Fred and answered for myself.

"He hung himself in Chicago," I tell Susan.

"And you feel on an energetic level?" Susan queried.

"I *think*, Chicago, and he sends me images. I can see him hanging by a rope." It's shocking but also a relief for me to *know* the answer.

The end of the session draws to a close. Susan asked if I wanted more visits from my ancestors, and I did. I tell the ancestors to come visit me however they will.

It has been nine years since my first hypnotherapy session. I still speak with the ancestors in my dreams. They don't visit with the same frequency, but their intentions are clear when they do come around.

Author's Note

Every family has its secrets and shame; those troubling stories that persist through time. Tales are passed down, whispered from grandmother to granddaughter, and these legends become so ingrained in our minds that we forget to question why they happened. Or better yet, could they have been prevented in the first place? It is impossible to know what will make one person stronger and what will break someone else altogether. One sibling flourishes while the other teeters on the edge of despair. The strange events surrounding the disappearance of my great-grandfather is one such story. Unwittingly, Fred Woodworth shaped generations with a single act.

We descendants all have our own opinions about what happened to him, but none of us ever knew for sure. When I was a child, I remember my mother saying perhaps he'd run off to South America to start a new life. I recently found a newspaper article that stated the same supposition. Some thought he'd committed suicide, and possibly his mother had suggested it as the best way out of the mess he'd made. It seemed more romantic to imagine my great-grandfather living south of the equator than to think of him ending his life in a small hotel room in the Midwest. It is rumored that Abby took her eldest son by buggy to the station, put him on a train, and he was never seen again. I wondered if he had been planning his exit, perhaps hiding money to finance his new life. When all was said and done, and he'd disappeared, I suspect someone close to Fred knew the real truth. I believe this person hid the facts from the family and the rest of the world, and took them with them to their grave.

The legacy of my mother's family was tucked away for generations, waiting to be uncovered. Its endowment wasn't wealth, or property, or business holdings. The gift, as I understand it now, was discovery. There were clues in the scraps of paper with scribbled lineages, newspaper clippings, letters, photographs, and stories. This delicate ephemera was so much more valuable than monetary gain—I was granted lost history and the joy of knowing those people whose DNA runs through me. I'm grateful to be the one it was bestowed upon, and I am convinced I was compelled to write our story by powers far greater than myself.

I wanted to write about my mother's life as I knew it, but I heard a small voice persistently whispering: *To understand your mother, you must first know her people and the land where they lived and worked and loved. Only then will the generations past and present experience healing.* And then I knew I had to go much further back to really learn and understand her.

Once I came to grips with the idea that the ancestors would tell me everything I needed to know, the following steps were to remain open to the meanderings of our story and let the path unfold with care. I put myself in their shoes, and previously unknown motivations came to light. I began to recognize patterns in the ways they coped with profound losses and how exuberant were their expressions of love and joy.

Despite everything I learned of my predecessors, it was impossible to perceive, without a shadow of doubt, what was in their minds. The people, places, and events in my story contain as much of the truth as I could uncover, and the rest is what I believe or was able to conjure.

To those of my family wondering about the family trees included in this book, please know that I could not include all of Abijah's siblings. There was a decision to cut it from 10 children to 7. You also might wonder why those dearly departed are listed as living. I did this because as of the end of this fictional account, those ancestors of ours were still living. Do you understand now how time and history and fiction have played havoc with my mind?

For anyone interested in learning more about the real family members, I invite you to have a look at a small gallery of photos on my website: https://amygirlwrites.com/the-secret-lives-of-ancestors.

This journey has illuminated the person I am in ways I could never have imagined. I have been told my ancestors chose me as their instrument to heal past trauma, and I agreed wholeheartedly to this considerable task.

I am the archive.

-AmyLee
November 20, 2024

About the Author

AmyLee is the author of *Bird with a Bright Object* and *More Bright and Shiny Things*. Her raw verses are filled with the grit of life and love.

She also writes of personal essays, memoir, flash and micro-fiction, which can be found on her Medium site: https://medium.com/@amylee_53969. She's worked in the book and publishing world for decades, and now spends her days writing and supporting other independent authors.

AmyLee lives in the Foothills of California with her husband and is a long-time member of the Sonora Writers' Group. Contact her via her website at https://amygirlwrites.com/

Milton Keynes UK
Ingram Content Group UK Ltd.
UKHW030703251124
3094UKWH00035B/200

9 798986 083841